Don't Call Me Iron Man

By

N.D. Wylders

A Beyond Fairytales Adaptation

of

The Brothers' Grimm Tale of Iron John

Don't Call Me Iron Man
Cover art by Syneca Featherstone

Published by Decadent Publishing Company, LLC
Look for us online at:

~Dedication~

A special thanks goes out to all my critiquing partners, those wonderful women who take the time to hold my hand as I slaved over this story. Gloria, Amanda, and Yvette, you girls rock! Also I can't say thank you enough to Dena who helped me with all the wonderful BDSM terms and practices. Your advice was invaluable.

Prologue

"Yo, Iron Man!"

Ivan Chugunov stilled by the door of Paddy McFee's, a local Irish pub located just a few blocks from his work. He scanned the crowded bar for a familiar face to match the voice. Dante, the dark-haired culprit, wore his trademark black fedora as he waved from his spot near the upright piano. Ivan gave Dante the one-fingered salute before shrugging out of his jacket.

"How many times do I have to tell that asshole not to call me Iron Man? I'm not some damn superhero." He hung his leather bomber on the coat rack then stepped up to the bar and took a seat. The owner and resident barkeep, Shamus O'Connor, smiled from behind the long expanse of polished teak. After drawing a mug of Ivan's favorite draft AmberBock, Shamus set the frosty glass on a napkin in front of him.

"I reckon if you want the lad to quit a'calling you names, you might wanna shave off your fancy facial hair." Shamus chuckled as he wiped a nonexistent splatter from the bar with the white towel draped over his shoulder.

Ivan rubbed his goatee. Shave it off? Not in this lifetime. It covered the large port-wine birthmark on his chin. Besides, he'd worn it a helluva lot longer than those damned Iron Man movies had been out.

"Shamus, it's not just the Tony Stark mustache and beard. It's his attitude." Dante sidled up to the bar along with his lover, Ronan.

Ronan smiled up at Ivan. "Naw, it's not just the facial hair. It's all those crazy inventions he comes up with." He tapped Ivan's arm. "Dad told me the other day you designed another new part which is supposed to revolutionize the security industry."

Ivan's cheeks warmed. Ronan's father had worked with him at Herman's & Sons Security Services since the day they'd hired him. For a long time, he'd been Ivan's mentor and teacher, and with Ivan moving into one of the coveted senior tech jobs, the man always bragged to anyone who would listen about his "protégé's" accomplishments.

"No offense, Ronan, but your dad thinks the same about every new project I work on. Once you finish your fancy degree, you'll put my little inventions to shame." He shifted on the barstool, uncomfortable with the accolades. He invented to satisfy his own curiosity and pay his bills, not bask in the limelight.

"As if." Ronan sighed and shook his head, before lifting up onto his toes to give Dante a kiss. "Later, babe. Have a good set. I'll keep the sheets warm for you." Then he disappeared into the crowd.

Shamus rapped the counter, signaling another order was up to the barmaid who appeared next to Ivan. As soon as the waitress left with the order, Shamus turned back to Ivan. "Perhaps one day the boy will do great things, but he'll never be you, Ivan. Face it, you're a true Iron Man—money, high IQ, and all. Whether you want to be or not."

"I suppose. But, at least, Iron Man gets to go home with Pepper at the end of the day. All I have is a demon-spawn, calico feline waiting for me." The joke was lame, but it hid his loneliness. *Time to change the subject.* Ivan grabbed his beer. "I'm gonna go play some darts before the boards get too busy." He glanced at Dante. "If you have time later, why don't you join me? I haven't kicked your ass in a while."

Dante chuckled. "Sure thing. I'm a glutton for punishment. Besides, Ronan has an early test tomorrow, so he'll be in bed long before I get home."

"Catch you then." He pushed away from the bar. As he made his way back to the small game room, several of the regulars hollered at him. Other than a few brief nods, he didn't stop to talk. Few would take him up on his offer for a game of cricket. His reputation as a brutal dart player proceeded him. But, later, after Dante finished his set on the piano, he looked forward to trouncing his friend on the boards. Until then, he'd warm up and take a quick breather from the noise of the rapidly filling bar. Even the quiet back room was better than his empty apartment. For the past few years, no one other than Luci-belle had waited for his return at the end of the day. No boyfriend, no lover, in fact no other human had crossed his threshold since Jackson had decided he'd had enough and left. Nope, now it was just him and a cat whose only interest was in Ivan's ability to work the can opener.

He gave a sigh of relief as he slipped inside the small room, off the back of the bar, without being stopped. The room housed Shamus's Friday night poker tournaments, along with three old, battered dartboards hung on the far wall. He left his beer on the edge of the poker table before he made his way over to his favorite corkboard. As he pulled out the steel-tipped darts, he felt the presence of someone behind him. Without turning, he assumed it was Dante or one of his other friends.

"If you've come in here to razz me some more about those damned movies before your set, just leave."

"I can't say I know much about Iron Man or that Tony Stark fellow. But Iron John? It's a tale I'm all too familiar with."

As Ivan turned, the sounds of the bar faded away. Less than three feet from him, smack-dab in the middle of the poker table, sat the oddest little…man he'd ever seen. With green woolen britches, a long red tunic, and a mischievous twinkle in his eyes, the man had the appearance of a wizened old gnome. The fellow couldn't have been more than three-and-a-half feet tall. Ivan had come across a lot of strange things in his thirty-five-plus years, but he'd never ever seen anything quite as bizarre. Then, an electric-blue tarantula crawled from the man's bramble of a beard and climbed up to settle on his shoulder.

"Where the hell did you come from?" Ivan squeezed the darts in his hand, his heart thudding in his chest. A crackle of change was in the air. One Ivan wasn't certain he wanted any part of.

"Here. There." The man shrugged and ran his fingers over the spider's back. "Everywhere. Nowhere.

Take your pick." The arachnid vibrated before settling down. "Name's Nicodemus and storytelling is my game." The gnome's shrewd gaze seemed to weigh Ivan's worth before the odd fellow spoke again. "But the question is, are you worthy of the tale?"

Ivan wondered if he should be insulted or intrigued by the man's taunt. Curiosity won over irritation. "What tale?"

"The one of Iron John. Pay attention, lad!"

Amused by the man's outburst, Ivan pulled out one of the chairs and sat down mere inches from him. What would it hurt to humor the old guy? "Okay, I haven't heard a fairytale since I was a boy. Perhaps you could take my mind off my problems for a while."

"That be the spirit." Nicodemus winked at him. "But first, there be my price."

"You want payment?" Ivan arched a brow. The man had interrupted his game of darts, and now he wanted to be paid?

Stroking his hand down his gray beard, Nicodemus sighed. "Of course, nothing in life is free, my boy."

A smile tugged at Ivan's lips. "Very true. There's no such thing as a free lunch, as my momma always said." He pulled out a handful of change and a few folded ones then laid them on the table. "Will this be enough?"

Instead of answering, the storyteller snapped his fingers, and the tarantula jumped from its perch. The spider nipped one of the gold dollar coins Ivan carried for the vending machines at work between his jaws then scurried back to his master.

"And so it begins." Nicodemus's eyes brightened as he launched into his tale. "It all happened a long time ago, in a realm far away."

Ivan tipped his chair back, took a long draw off his beer, and chuckled as the room grew warmer while the light began to dim. Damn, had Shamus slipped something in his drink? It took some effort, but he managed to keep his eyes open and focused on the storyteller. "Don't you mean once upon a time?"

"Indeed."

Nicodemus sounded farther away, when the storyteller, his blue tarantula, the bar, and even the beer in his hand disappeared, as Ivan surrendered to the darkness.

Chapter One

Drip. Drip. Drip.

Groaning, Ivan rolled into an upright position. His ears rang to the steady beat of water hitting porcelain. Under him, a firm mattress cradled his body, while his head felt as if some sadistic bastard had let loose an evil anvil-pounding imp bent on driving him insane. *Exactly how much did I drink?* His mouth was drier than the Sahara in August. He pressed the heels of his hands against his achy temples. Dear Lord, he'd give anything to make it stop.

A low hiss escaped his parted lips as the leaky faucet continued to drip. The sound tortured his ears, even as it offered the possibility of relief to his parched tongue and throat. Attempting to stand, he swayed on his weakened knees. He thrust his arm out to brace himself. A grimace crossed his face at the cold, slimy surface under his palm. It took some effort, but he managed to open his eyes. At first, he saw nothing but shadows then the blurred lines of gray took shape. A slow turn of his aching head revealed the rest of the barren, cave-like room. He was surrounded by rock walls. There were no windows. Not even an obvious door. Nothing save a coarsely made cot against one wall, dirt-strewn floors, and in one corner, a stand with a chipped bowl placed beneath a leaky pipe.

"What the fuck?" He gritted his teeth as the room spun once then righted itself. "Goddamn, what did you put in my beer, old man?" He tried to remember how he'd gotten here in this little cell, or whatever the hell they wanted to call it. His last recollection was...paying some crazy little gnome with a blue tarantula to tell him a goddamned fairytale. Had the spider bitten him? Or maybe it had been the gnome who'd drugged him.

"Great. Either I drank too much, or a three-and-a-half-foot gnome kidnapped me."

But even as he attempted to decide which was the more likely, the water continued to torment him.

Drip. Drip. Drip.

Unable to ignore his needs any longer, he staggered over to the stand with the help of the wall. He fell to his knees in front of it. Lifting the basin with shaking hands, he spilled half of the precious liquid down the front of his polo shirt before getting more than a swallow or two into his mouth. The water soothed his tongue, but had an odd taste similar to well water. It didn't stop him though as he gulped at the cool essence until there was no more. With the worst of his thirst sated, he placed the bowl back under the pipe and waited for it to fill again.

By the time he'd drunk a second time, the evil anvil man had disappeared, only to leave a vague achiness in his wake. Now without his head pounding, maybe he could figure out why the hell he was in a cell. The probability of the gnome kidnapping him was illogical. The man wouldn't have had the strength to move a man his size. Perhaps it was Shamus or Dante playing another one of their practical jokes? If so, he would kick their asses the next time he saw them. But, first, he needed to get out—well, as soon as he was a bit steadier on his feet. He rested a few more minutes with his head and shoulders pressed back against the stone. After a while, he noticed there was recessed lighting in the ceiling.

"Lights? If there are lights, there has to be electricity, and if there's electricity, there has to be a way out of this room."

He struggled to his feet. He touched every crevice in the walls he could reach until his fingernails caught on the edge of a concealed compartment. Crouching, he tugged on it, but it refused to give. In a dim hope whoever had locked him up hadn't searched him, he

11

patted the front right pocket of his pants. He touched the familiar outlines of his Swiss Army knife and Zippo lighter. Thankful for the oversight, he fished out his multi-tool.

"Guess they didn't think to search me. Bad for them, but good for me."

After choosing the flathead-screwdriver attachment, it took him less than two minutes to snap the small hinges holding the cover on. He ignored the crash it made as it hit the ground. With the end of his knife, he prodded and poked at the wires inside the panel. Color coded, they were wrapped in a familiar configuration. In fact, it resembled one of the custom-wiring panels he'd created for an experimental electronic lock.

With a quick prayer, he eased apart the wire bundle until he found the two wires he needed. Using the knife, he cut them. A quick pass with his lighter loosened the sheaths, and he stripped away the outer casings. Once they were exposed, he twisted the ends together. Less than five seconds later, the cleverly concealed door slid open with a low hiss. He dropped the wires and straightened. "Easier than hotwiring my momma's old Chevy."

After a quick glance in both directions, he stepped out into the darkened corridor. Like the cell, it offered nothing hinting at his location. Deciding it probably wouldn't matter in the end, he took a step to the left then froze when a huge brute of a man appeared out of the darkness. Dressed in stained leather pants, thick-heeled boots, and a frayed tunic shot through with metallic threads, the stranger cast a rather imposing figure. Adding the worn-leather bracelets at both wrists and the thick belt with a short blunt sword, the man's stout build suggested he was lethal as well.

Unease pooled in Ivan's stomach as the man spotted him.

"How did you get out? Queen Theria will not be pleased."

Ivan almost swallowed his tongue when the man closed the distance between them. Had he been cast into some kind of Medieval reenactment, complete with executioner? The bastard was even bigger than he was. He forced himself to remain calm.

"The magic touch?" Ivan held up his hands while balancing his weight on the balls of his feet. With drawn breath, Ivan waited for the other man to attack.

"Then the queen must know of this magic. Come with me. We must go to the Queen's Hall." The man palmed the hilt of his sword.

Ivan weighed his options. He might be smart, but he wasn't egotistical enough to think he could take on a man with a sword just his bare hands. "All right. I'll come." He skirted around the guard then followed the man's muttered directions. Several minutes later, they arrived outside of a pair of huge oak doors.

Whatever Ivan expected when he entered the Queen's Hall, it wasn't what he got. Instead of tapestries, velvets and brocades, and majestic furnishings, the room presented a blend of futuristic design with shiny-metal walls, vertical blinds, and uncomfortable-looking furniture. The floor gleamed underfoot and appeared to be polished stainless steel. At the center of the room, behind a sleek desk, a woman dipped the end of a long feather quill into a small metallic inkwell then scribbled on the pages of a massive book. The contrast of the futuristic, ultra-modern appearances with the outdated past of inkwells and quill pens caused Ivan to doubt his senses. Where in the hell was he?

The guard cleared his throat and the woman glanced up, her expression far from serene. Her eyes narrowed in obvious irritation at the interruption, the bags under them more pronounced than he expected. She pursed her lips, and her eyebrows drew together before she relaxed her face. The quick metamorphosis baffled him while sending the urge to flee to his folded limbs. *This* was the queen?

As she stood, Ivan struggled to reconcile this woman with any fairytale version of a queen he'd ever read about. But it was impossible. She didn't have the appearance of a matriarch. Tall, like the guard, her blonde hair was pixie short and shot through with a bit of gray. She wore knee-high leather boots and a form-fitting black jumper. The only outward sign of her rule were the precious jewels adorning each shoulder, the silver chain accenting her slender waist, and the huge opaque stone nestled in a wide silver ring on the middle finger of her left hand. But even without a crown or scepter, her aura of power was palpable.

"Milady, begging your pardon." The guard dropped to one knee then dragged Ivan down to kneel next to him. He grunted when the man slapped the back of his head forward into a bow. Out of the corner of his eye, Ivan watched the guard do the same. No matter the queen's appearance, the guard made his expectations pretty clear. Ivan would respect his queen or he wasn't above using brute force to push the issue.

"I know you asked for the intruder to remain locked away, but, during my rotations, I found him in the hall outside his cell."

"And why did you not put him back inside it, Caroc?" The click of her heels against the floor echoed through the room.

"I would've, milady, but I wasn't sure how he got out. The door was shut."

"Really?" As she moved closer, the click of her heels grew louder. "Then we do have a mystery here, since only Master Aranos and I have keys to the cells."

Placing a finger under Ivan's chin, she tilted it up. Her shrewd eyes—crystalline blue with a rim of gray, dissected him as if he were under a magnifying glass. "You were unconscious when my guards found you outside the north gate. What is your name?"

"Ivan Chugunov."

"Did you steal Master Aranos's key, Mr. Chugunov?"

"I stole nothing." Ivan spoke softly.

"Really? We shall see." She released him to turn toward the second guard who rushed into the room. "Call for Master Aranos."

The idea she thought him a thief rankled. "I stole nothing. If you didn't want me to get out, you should've taken my utility knife."

In a single move, she thrust her hand out to clutch his throat. She squeezed once in warning then leaned in until her nose touched his.

The guard sprang to his feet then drew his long sword and stepped behind him. Ivan froze at the touch of steel against the base of his neck.

"You dare bring a weapon into the Queen's Hall?" she hissed.

It was hard to speak, but he managed. "It's harmless."

She tightened her grip. "I'll be the judge of that. Where is it?"

A low growl built in his chest. If it hadn't been for the sword tip resting between his shoulder blades, Ivan would've pushed her hand aside. "Front pocket." He kept his gaze on her as her guard's hand plunged into the pockets of his loose pants.

"Nothing, milady, other than this." Caroc opened his hand to reveal the familiar red pocket knife with a white cross on it.

The queen glanced at it, before she returned her attention to him. "That is a weapon?"

Ivan shook his head. "No. A multi-tool. I used it to open the door."

She pursed her lips. "You can control energy?" She dropped her hand.

"Control, no; manipulate, yes."

For the first time since he'd been in her presence, something other than irritation filled her gaze. It resembled hope. Then, she narrowed her eyes. "You will show me."

He swallowed hard, but nodded as Caroc dragged him to his feet. Would this nightmare ever end?

A short time later found him back in the dungeons, this time with the queen in attendance. However, instead of returning him to his original cell, they placed him in a different one. As soon as the door slid shut, he repeated the process.

When the door slid open, Queen Theria's face was filled with wonder. "You're the answer to my prayers. You shall use this gift to save my people."

"Excuse me? I don't see how being able to hotwire a cell door will help you." He raked his hand through his hair. "Unless, of course, you have a tendency to lock yourself out of your...." He searched for a word to describe the space around him. "House?"

She drew a hard breath in, scowling at him. "No one would dare lock me out of the Great Hall. What I need is your way with energy. Since the disappearance of our LT-1789 unit, there has been no one in our clutch who can manipulate the circuitry that cleans our water or runs my home. You will locate it and bring it back here. If you don't, you'll die."

Ivan stilled. "You'll kill me? Forgive me, but I believe murder is still illegal in the United States."

She shook her head. "I know nothing of this United States. You are in Krontos, the ruling clutch of Sisera, in the Fourth Realm. And it will not be I who kills you, but the poisons inside your body."

Sisera? The Fourth Realm?

The woman had to have a screw loose. Why hadn't some nice men with a handy white straitjacket already hauled her away?

"However, you can avoid such a terrible fate if you help us." She continued to pace.

"I can?"

"Yes. The parasites within us have begun to make my people sick. The only thing protecting us was a water purifier that no longer works. Along with the loss of our medical unit, we are living on borrowed time. That's where you come in."

Dread pooled in his stomach, but he decided to play along. "So if I fix the purifier, then bring back this LT-whatever, it will save your people."

"We believe so." She sighed. "Our world is being consumed. Or so my advisors tell me. The An'tealan Forest has encroached on us for several generations. Before, we were able to keep it at bay, but...." An unreadable emotion crossed her face. "Since my reign began, we've failed. The forest is no longer passable. We are cut off from our sister clutches and have to rely on what we can salvage. So, unless you can turn the purifier back on and retrieve the LT-1789, our time is limited. Even if I could send you back, the parasites already within you would probably kill you."

Ivan closed his eyes. He'd play along for now. But, the first chance he got, he'd escape. "So, if I get the water purifier working and find the medical unit, you will give me the cure and then send me back to Chicago?"

She nodded. "Of course. If my advisors are able to find a way, I shall return you to your Chicago."

***

"How much longer?" Caroc asked for the tenth time as he moved closer. "It will soon be dark, and the An'tealan Forest is no place to be once the sun sets."

"Dammit, I don't know! Stand back! You're blocking my light. It'll be fixed when it gets fixed." Ivan glared at the four guards behind him before returning to his task. After a two-hour trek into the dense woods with four shadows, his patience was gone. Kneeling in front of an antiquated machine attached to a half-submerged waterwheel, he'd finally located what he hoped was the main circuit board. Unlike the cell's electronic lock, it had taken more time and substantial effort to remove the access panel. The vegetation around the unit had made his job nearly impossible, not just difficult. Once he'd hacked through the stranglehold the greenery had on the machine, it had become the guards' constant hovering which pissed him off. They were in his way, even Caroc. Didn't they realize crowding him wouldn't fix the machine any faster?

He pushed aside another bundle of wires then grinned as he spotted the circuit board. It was free of rust and other contaminants. *Now, to check the connections.* Tilting it toward the fading light, he examined each wire connected to the board.

Everything was in its proper place order, but where the hell was the power source? When he couldn't find one, he again dug back into the innards at the base of the old equipment. A triumphant sound passed his lips as he found the loose wire inside the bottom of the machine.

After reconnecting it around the small screw used to anchor it, he placed the board back inside, and began to press random buttons on the front panel of the machine. It took several tries, but he found a working one. The dirty display screen lit up as the machine hiccupped, hissed, and then grumbled to life. The small paddle wheel next to the machine gave a lurch. Ivan gave a small shout of accomplishment. "Turn, you bitch."

The meter on the screen continued to rise as water flowed through the machine, until it gave a beep as the filter kicked in. "Looks like it's fixed. It seems to be sustaining water pressure."

"You did it! Queen Theria will be so pleased." Caroc turned to two of the other men. "Return to her at once and give her the good news. Rancor and I will set up camp for the night. Inform her we will begin our search for the LT-1789 tomorrow morning."

The other two guards nodded and disappeared from Ivan's sight.

He rose and faced the remaining guards after replacing and securing the panel. Maybe he could escape tonight once they slept. But until then, he had to let them think he'd follow orders. He pasted a smile on his face.

"Okay boys, what else can I do to help? I don't know about you, but I am hungry."

A few hours later, with a full stomach, Ivan pretended to settle in for the night. It hadn't taken him and the two guards long to make camp. Soon after he'd fixed the machine, they'd had a fire built. While he and Caroc set up the small pup tents, the other guard had managed to catch some kind of fish Ivan had never seen before for their meal. Not that he had ever been up close and personal with a fish before it'd entered his mouth. He was a product of his urban upbringing and modern grocery stores. Now, he listened to the crickets and the frogs croak while he waited for the other men to settle in for the night. He wondered how much longer it would be when a sudden scream pierced the night air. It was followed by the sound of breaking branches, grunts, and curses from the two guards. Were they being attacked by a bear?

"Help me!" The agonized plea was eclipsed by footsteps.

Horrified, Ivan threw open the flap on his tent and palmed his small penlight. Even if he was their hostage, he couldn't very well let a bear eat them. He scrambled free of the tent's small confines then almost gagged. It was no bear. Almost eight feet tall, it had scales, long ebony tusks, and five-inch claws. *It's like some reject from a* Creature Feature. In the dappled moonlight, the grotesque monster stood upright on two feet as it tossed Caroc into the air like a toy. As the man plummeted to the earth, it caught him between its jaws. Snapping, razor-sharp teeth shut around the guard's thick shoulder, the beast shook the man.

Caroc's scream pierced the night as razor-sharp talons raked open the man's vulnerable stomach. Blood spurted, and Ivan stumbled back. The flight instinct was riding him hard. Nothing could've prepared him for the brutality of the attack. Or the grim reality he most definitely was not in Kansas anymore.

"Be still." The sudden harsh whisper filled his ear.

Already on edge, Ivan jumped. A soft curse passed his lips as he was dragged back against a hard body. His penlight revealed the planes of an almost perfect face before the device was knocked out of his hand to the ground. Surprise warred with apprehension as the other man held him with ease then closed a dark cloak of some type around their combined bodies. Ivan tried to twist away, but his captor refused to let him go, even when he arched backward and ground his ass against the stranger's groin. Within moments, the man's cock stiffened then wedged between the cheeks of Ivan's ass.

A hand clamped over his hip. "Stop. Now is *not* the time to lure me with your wicked ways. I don't care what the queen has promised you. It will matter not if we don't survive. The *morte'metentis* has an unshakable thirst for human blood, but has poor vision. Our only chance to survive is to remain still. It may not be able to see us, but it has sharp hearing."

"It does?" He cringed at the sound of bones crunching when the beast tore an arm from the guard's mangled, limp body. Even though he didn't care for Caroc, he wouldn't have wished such a fate on him.

"Yes. Now be still. I do not wish to be its dessert." Then, as if the mysterious stranger could read his mind, the man spoke again. "There is nothing we can do for him. Even a drop of its venom is fatal for humans. He was dead from the moment it tagged him."

Ivan had no choice but to stand still in the man's arms, as the *morte'metentis* devoured the last of its late-night snack. Each growl, as the beast shredded its feast, seared into his memory. His utter helplessness warred with desperation. There would be no escape for him. He didn't know how it had happened, but he wasn't on Earth anymore. And he would have to play Queen Theria's game if he wanted to go home. But without his guard, how could he even find the missing medic unit or return to the clutch? *I'm so fucked.*

Chapter Two

Holding the man, while a wild *morte'metentis* devoured one of the guards of his former clutch, was about the height of stupidity to Lucero. The entire scene smacked of Queen Theria's handiwork. *Only she would endanger her own men.* The An'tealan Forest was beyond dangerous once night fell. He should've never allowed himself to be drawn to the old purification site at dusk—it was more than likely a trap. But the hum from the purifier had been irresistible. Its sound alone, as it began pumping, had drawn him from the safety of his home.

While he'd kept to the shadows, it'd been too late by the time he'd arrived. He'd been unable to help as the large predator ripped the small campsite apart in search of food. It devoured canvas, fiberglass poles, and human flesh alike. There was no reasoning with the mindless beast either. All he could do was be still and watch. As the animal tore apart the first man, a second one fled. He'd mumbled a quick prayer under his breath for their souls. Even a baby *morte'metentis* would track the other fool with ease. Although

Lucero's enhanced hearing pinpointed the escapee's path, even a human could hear the fool crashing through the woods. He'd just turned away from the carnage when a small pinpoint of light illuminated the last standing tent—a beacon in the darkness. He wanted to scream out a warning, but fear paralyzed him as the beast pivoted toward the narrow shaft of luminescence.

The scaly monster tossed away the remains of the guard, its roar goading him to action. Lucero's heart jumped as he sprang forward. He couldn't in good conscience let the man die. He slipped from the shadows and knocked the small penlight to the ground while drawing the large man into the black depths of his cloak. After a very brief struggle between them, while the unseeing beast returned to its meal, he waited impatiently. Unfortunately, he'd also inhaled the slight musky smell of the other man. He'd been surprised the stranger had given in so easily, but perhaps he knew of Queen Theria's ruthless behavior. It wasn't until the *morte'metentis* had finished its destruction then disappeared into the tree line and he released the man, that he got his first good glance at him.

In the dim light of fire, he made out a face so familiar to him he almost fell to his knees. *Vihaan—the queen's son!*

"How can this be?" He swallowed hard then lifted his hand toward the man. "You can't be here. You're dead. *Sisera* reclaimed your soul over two years ago, and they set your body aflame and onto the next realm." He backpedaled when the man knocked his arm away.

"Next realm? What the hell are you talking about? My name is Ivan Chugunov, and I'm very much alive." The man's form was backlit by the fire which revealed broad shoulders, a long torso, slim waist, and powerful thighs. It was enough to make Lucero's mouth water. "I'm from Chicago, and let me assure you, all I want to do is to go home."

Lucero wet his lower lip as he fought to control his reawakened libido. "And where is home? The royal clutch?"

The man scowled. "Willingly stay with the crazy bitch—no, not even for a million bucks. I'm gonna find this stupid LT...whatever unit...and then I'll be on my way back to Earth."

Lucero's blood went cold at the mention of his scientific name. "What is this Earth you speak of, and how will this...medical unit insure your trip home? Has the bitch queen found a new way to cross dimensions?" Hope blossomed in him. If Theria had indeed found a way to cross time and space, Lucero might be tempted to strike up a bargain with her—if it meant he could be with Vihaan once more. His heart ached for his former lover.

The man laughed. "Not exactly. She said she'd have her advisors find a way to send me home if I fixed the purifier and also brought home this missing medical unit...."

As fast as his hopes had risen, they crashed. "I suggest you get used to the royal life. You'll be here for some time."

The man stalked toward the fire. "They will find a way to send me home." The desperation in his tone made Lucero wish he still held the man.

"If I were you, I wouldn't count on it." At his glare, Lucero shook his head. "Think about it. If they had to send you to fix a loose connection on a water purifier, how can you expect them to have the knowledge to find a way to return you to your world?"

The little hope Ivan clung to since he'd run from his tent slipped through his fingers. He narrowed his eyes at the cloak-covered figure. The man's animosity toward the queen was apparent. Perhaps it colored his view? "You lie. You hate the queen."

The shadowy figure moved closer to the fire. "To say there is no affection between us would be an understatement, but I wouldn't lie about something as important as this." He moved to the fire and kicked loose dirt over the dying embers.

"What are you doing?" Confusion swamped Ivan. The man wouldn't tell him the reason behind his hatred, and now he was taking away what little safety they had?

"Putting out the fire. I live in peace with Sisera and her forests when possible. To leave a fire unattended could have disastrous results."

Frustrated, he grabbed the covered arm of the man. "Why? The fire is all that stands between us and an attack! Do you want to get us both killed?"

He shrugged off his hand. "I do not plan to be here for another attack. I will not tempt Sisera twice in one night. It's only because of her good graces we will manage to escape the beast. I'm thankful it was only a baby. Mama would've ripped us to shreds. Now, please gather what you can't live without and follow me." The voice came from within the folds of the hood, hard, almost distant. His nonchalance indicated he didn't care which choice Ivan made.

"But...." Ivan grasped at straws, but didn't care. "Wait! What if the other guard comes back! Or what about the men sent back to the clutch? They are to return with fresh supplies in the morning."

From a distance, screams of agony then death ripped through the night air. Ivan cringed as the other man's head bowed.

"Either place your faith in foolish notions or follow me." The man turned. "You have three minutes to decide. Then I'm leaving—with or without you."

Panic began to build in the pit of Ivan's stomach. Should he stay with the fire and hope he could rebuild it before the animal came back? Or should he place his life in the hands of the strange male who'd already saved him once?

A loud snap echoed through the suddenly silent forest. It made his choice clear, as his rescuer straightened, his head turning toward the wood line. Ivan tried to see what had caught the man's attention. But even as he scanned their surroundings, he was unable to identify what caused the noise. It sent his already active imagination into overdrive. His nerves were tense, like a spring-loaded mousetrap, ready to snap at the slightest brush.

He stumbled backward, when the cloak-covered man spun in the opposite direction of the noise. Ivan's heart was in his throat when the man glanced over his shoulder.

"Decide!" he hissed. "Danger stalks us every moment we linger."

His choice made, Ivan cursed under his breath, and darted toward his tent. After snagging the battered bag, the queen had given him to carry his supplies, he returned to the man's side. While there was nothing of sentimental value inside it, the food and water it contained were essential. He wasn't a fool. The hard pressed meat, similar to pemmican, and a bag of some kind of odd nuts didn't taste the greatest, but would mean the difference living and starvation. "Okay, I'm ready. Lead on, Obi-wan."

The man stilled. "I know nothing of this, Obi-wan. I'm called Lucero."

The loud crash behind them sounded too close for comfort. He stumbled as his rescuer shoved him toward the tree line. "Keep to the shadows!"

Fear unlike anything he'd ever known raced through Ivan. "But what about you...."

"Damn it all!" A loud roar and the heavy thud of a stampeding animal shook the ground. "I will face the beast. Now, hide!"

Lucero spun and his cloak parted to give Ivan a glimpse of a pair of tight leather pants and a cream shirt. Unable to move, all he could do was watch in horror as Lucero drew the beast's attention with a sharp whistle. The monster shifted directions and attacked the other man.

As Lucero pitted his strength and agility against the predator, Ivan's legs were nothing more than lumps of clay. The memory of the prior attack was strong, until all he could foresee was the other man suffering the same fate. *And it's only a baby?* A low moan ripped free from him when Lucero darted to the left to avoid the *morte'metentis's* razor-like claws. In his hand, the dark outline of a knife flickered in the dim light before Lucero's arm sliced downward in a swift, vicious movement. A pained shriek escaped the animal as the knife's edge raked along its flank and drew blood.

Lucero danced backward when the wounded predator lunged at him. Ivan stared. He'd never seen a man move so quickly in his entire life. It was as if he weren't human. Each time the animal tried to claw at him, he managed to be just out of reach. Would his luck run out? He had to be tiring—no man could continue at this pace forever. Then Lucero would be at the mercy of the beast. He couldn't let him be ripped apart. Not after the man had saved his life, not once, but twice, tonight.

His heart racing, Ivan scanned the ground for a weapon. He dropped to his knees. His fingers dug at the packed dirt around a thick, gnarled branch. Five-feet long and several inches around, it would at least get the beast's attention. He rose, but tried to keep his movements hidden. With his impromptu weapon clenched between his fists, he clung to the shadows as he skirted the combatants.

Lucero's eyes widened when Ivan moved out of the shadows.

"No!" Lucero hissed. The *morte'metentis's* claws caught his bicep and scored the flesh. He clutched at his arm.

A dark-black substance oozed from the wound. Ivan's hotheaded Cossack blood demanded retribution, even as his brain tried to process what he saw. Lucero's blood or venom from the monster's claws?

Didn't matter. "Argh!" He swung with all his might and hit the beast's flank. The branch snapped with a crack as the animal roared in pain. "Not so funny now, is it, fucker?" Picking up the other half of the branch, he used both to pummel the injured animal until the *morte'metentis* shrieked and fled into the dense underbrush. Ivan bent over at the waist and gasped for breath, heart racing.

"You fool. I could've lost you again!" The hard tone was followed by an even harder hand yanking him up against Lucero's body. Before he could protest, the smaller man dragged his head down and captured his mouth in a punishing kiss.

Ivan froze for a moment. It'd been over two years since he'd felt another's mouth against his. He gave a muffled moan. The man tasted of something he could only liken to roasted pistachios as their tongues rubbed against one another. Unable to resist, he buried his hand in Lucero's hair and cupped the back of his head, as he took control of the kiss, or attempted to.

The other man freed himself with ease before staring at him through shuttered eyes, his lips swollen and wet. "Forgive me. I shouldn't have done that." He pushed away and tore a strip of fabric from the bottom of his shirt. After he wrapped it around his wounded arm, he tied it off. "Either come with me or don't. The choice is yours." He brushed past.

More than a little bit aroused, Ivan caught his good arm. "You shouldn't have what? Saved me, or kissed me?"

Lucero stared down at Ivan's hand. "Remove it or lose it. I am in no mood to be manhandled by a *stultus homo*." He jerked free of Ivan's grip to retrieve his cloak from the ground. With a flick of his fingers, he settled it over his wide shoulders and fastened the clasp. "I'm leaving."

***

Lucero called himself all kinds of a fool as he maneuvered through the thick An'tealan forest. He had gone to the purification site then been injured while saving a man who would be his downfall. Only his complex circuitry and nanos within his systems kept him from falling prey to the venom even now coursing through his veins. Too bad they couldn't protect him from Queen Theria. By ordering Ivan to return with him, it was obvious she still considered him little more than a fancy can opener she could use and abuse at will. "Never again," he muttered under his breath.

"What?" At his heels, it was the first time the larger man had spoken since they'd left the campsite. Ivan's lack of vocal communication should've pleased him, but still it managed to keep him off balance. Vihaan would've had filled the silence with continuous babble.

Ducking under a large branch of the *salicem*, Lucero pushed the wispy fronds away from his face. "Nothing. Duck." He tossed the command over his shoulder but didn't bother to see if the other man obeyed. It would serve Ivan right if he coldcocked himself on the low-hanging branch. Other than a low-muttered oath, the other man kept pace with him. "We'll be there soon. Hope you can climb."

A few minutes later, the large rock mound he'd built his home upon appeared. After he grabbed hold of the ladder fashioned out of the *tuerentur* fronds, he began to climb. It took less than three minutes for both of them to scale the rocks, but it seemed longer to him. Probably because he could feel the heavy weight of Ivan's gaze on his ass as he pulled himself up.

Once at the top, he threw his leg over the edge and grabbed the rough-hewn handrail he'd made from dried *salicem* branches. Lucero scrambled into an upright position then turned to offer Ivan a hand, but instead found his guest-to-be already straightening.

"Damn. It's amazing." Ivan stopped and gazed at the sprawled structure Lucero called home.

He couldn't help but experience a bit of pride at the other man's awe. He'd lugged up every single stone, every piece of wood, and woven by hand every frond holding his sanctuary together. Standing a mere ten feet in height, it was a combination of whatever he'd managed to scavenge from Sisera's bounty. Even the glass in the windows and the solar panels which powered his home had come from his clutch's abandoned buildings. But despite the modern amenities, he'd been determined to change the land as little as possible. It was the reason his home butted up against a sheer, towering cliff and was flanked by two huge *salicem* trees.

Ivan turned to Lucero. "Did you build all this?"

Lucero gave a short nod. "Over time. Come. Even elevated as we are, we're still not safe. There are predators just as lethal as the *morte'metentis* which can swoop down from the sky." He navigated the narrow, rocky path toward his home, avoiding the large *veneno* bushes. "Be careful not to touch the vegetation with the bluish-purple berries. A mere scratch from their thorns will put a man your size down for at least half a day."

"Got it. Don't touch the blueberry bushes." Ivan followed in his footsteps.

After he pressed his thumb on the scanner next to the door, Lucero waited the two seconds it took for its scan to release the lock then twisted the handle. Once inside his home, he hung his cloak on the peg by the door then headed toward the kitchen. His arm ached like a bitch.

In front of the sink, he turned on the tap and stripped off the makeshift bandage. After he dampened a clean rag, he began the tedious process of cleaning out the wound. A hiss escaped him when he realized the cut was deeper than he'd thought. The laceration exposed circuitry normally hidden underneath several layers of dense muscle. It would take more than a butterfly bandage to close the wound. He needed stitches. "Shit."

"Damn, I would've never expected this." Ivan appeared in the entryway of the dining area. "You must be quite handy with electronics."

Lucero kept his back to him. "One might say that." He ran another cool stream of water over the wound.

"In the cupboard next to the entry is a med kit. Grab it."

The rustling behind him assured Lucero the man had obeyed. Moments later the small metal box was set down on the narrow lip of the sink. "I need a hand. Inside there's sutures and a curved needle. I hope your stomach is strong. This will take more than a few stitches to close." At the continued silence, he glanced up at Ivan. The man stared at the exposed wires and circuit boards in his arm. "What?"

Ivan's lips thinned. "You're not human."

Chapter Three

Ivan stumbled back from the sink, as the accusation passed his lips. What he'd just seen couldn't be real, but the gouge, which exposed both wires and circuitry inside human tissues, wouldn't go away, even when he rubbed his eyes. Then he remembered the other man's endurance and speed during the fight with the *morte'metentis*. Panic grew as things started to add up, and in a way he didn't like. *But what other explanation can there be? A man of Lucero's size shouldn't have been able to haul the materials up here to build his home. Even with a pulley system, it would've been a two-person job.* But if Lucero was a machine, why would he even want a home?

Lucero exhaled. "I won't hurt you. In fact, my moral code forbids it. I'm a cybernetic medical unit. The LR-1789 unit the queen sent you after. However, I'm not a machine. I'm a human who's been enhanced in several ways to heal the royal clutch. And, at this moment, I'm bleeding all over the place. If you want a chance at finishing your mission, I suggest you get over here and help me because, unlike machines, I can die."

Ivan clenched his jaw, but moved closer. *"You're* the LR-1789?"

He sighed and gave a short nod. "I prefer Lucero to that ridiculous number."

A pinched expression crossed the cyborg's face when Ivan turned his arm over to examine the wound. His intellectual curiosity kicked into place, as he examined the hair-thin fibers threaded through the muscle tissue to connect a series of tiny microchips to a much larger circuit board. He couldn't tell if there was damage to the connections or not because of the thick purplish-green liquid around the wound. "I've never dealt with a cyborg before. Are your veins organic or cybernetic?"

Lucero jerked his arm away. "What does it matter? I need you to sew me up. Not ask me a million questions about my anatomy."

Surprised by the outburst, he hauled Lucero's arm back toward him. *A machine with emotions? Or an imitation of them?* "You want me to fix you up or not? I need to know what I'm dealing with. If you lose too much *blood*, will I have to make a run to the local hardware store for a can of oil, or will I have to open a vein to give you a transfusion?"

Lucero gave him a *let's get this fucking done* look as he pushed the tin closer to Ivan, his intent obvious. "While I'm not sure what this hardware store is, I assure you the only oil in my home is for cooking. I'm an enhanced human, not an android. Other than the tech surgically implanted in my body, I'm as *organic* as you. You should've realized that when I started to bleed. It was just sheer bad luck the damned *morte'metentis* damaged the area around my evaluation port. If his claws had struck two *proculs* lower, he'd have shredded me to the bone, and I would've bled out before anything could have been done."

Ivan opened the tin box then glanced up at his patient. "Chill out. I don't know how you expected me to react, but where I come from, we don't have cyborgs outside of motion pictures. Nor do we have sentient beings who are half-man, half-machine. It's either man or machine, not a combination of them, so excuse me for not realizing I'd offend your delicate sensibilities."

A low growl escaped the other man. "Delicate sensibilities? Considering I just got sliced up saving your ass, one would think you'd be a little bit more *appreciative*."

Ivan shrugged, pawing through the meager supplies in front of him. "So I didn't say thank you. I was in shock. I never expected to be attacked by some animal straight out of Jurassic Park. Even if I had, a bad-assed cyborg to the rescue wasn't in my plan." When he found no actual bandages or towels, he shed his T-shirt and used it to dry the cyborg's arm. "Give me a second, and I'll patch you up." Picking up a small brown bottle labeled *Antiseptic Spray*, he glanced up at Lucero. "Will this damage your circuitry?"

Lucero shook his head.

"Good to know. With the parasites in the water, I hoped you had either alcohol or hydrogen peroxide." Ivan opened a package of sterile gauze then used it to dab at the wound. The analytical side of his brain noticed the deep furrows in the center of the larger circuit board. His inner geek wondered what effect the gouges would have on the other man's performance, but the last thing he wanted was to piss Lucero off again. "So what exactly does this evaluation port do?"

"It...." Lucero hissed as Ivan pressed harder on the wound to staunch the flow of dark fluid seeping from the cut. "Fuck, that hurts...." He drew a deep breath. "It scans whatever I place on the skin above it. Then it sends a message...."

Beads of sweat popped out on Lucero's forehead when Ivan sprayed antiseptic into the wound. "To?" He grabbed another square of gauze to wipe off the extra spray and reached for the slightly curved needle and thin, almost translucent thread.

"To my brain pan. Ninety percent of my brain has been enhanced. I can analyze and create everything from healing poultices to antidotes to vaccines."

Ivan paused to thread the needle. "Including one to counteract the parasites in the water?"

Lucero nodded. "If I had a sample of the polluted water. Out here, Sisera is once again pure. Only those who live in the clutches still have parasites. Something to do with the minerals our technology puts off. After we lost her husband to them, I suggested the queen move her clutch. That everyone would continue to worsen and, if she didn't, I would take her son, Vihaan, away with me." A rueful smile crossed his face. "She laughed at me. Told me she would never abandon her home, and I was a fool if I thought Vihaan would give up his position as her heir to live with me in the godforsaken forest with no modern conveniences."

"Vihaan. Isn't that what you called me during the attack?"

"You could be his twin. Except for the hair on your face. He never wore a beard. No royalty ever does. It's the mark of a commoner. Or so the queen says."

Once he got the needle threaded, Ivan glanced up at his pale face. "You okay?"

"Yeah." Lucero clenched his jaw. "Just stitch the damned thing up."

Ivan nodded. "Okay." He rested the injured arm against the edge of the sink. "Here we go. I'll try not to hurt you too much...."

"It's gonna sting either way. Just do it." Then Lucero braced himself against the counter, as Ivan pushed the tip of the needle through the surprisingly warm skin.

***

"So let me get this straight. You paid some lawn ornament a dollar to tell you a story then blacked out, and woke up in Queen Theria's cell?" Lucero leaned back in the rocker, his hands folded across his stomach. His arm still throbbed from where his guest had stitched him up, but the pain was tolerable since he'd drunk some *tuerentur*-laced tea. While the fronds were strong and sturdy when woven together, the oil pressed from the ripe fruit was a wonderful painkiller.

"I guess when you put it that way, it does sound crazy." Ivan shifted on the thick pallet in front of the hearth. "All I know I was at my favorite pub in Chicago, shooting darts and having a beer after work then this storyteller appears and offers to tell me a tale. Next thing I know, I'm in another realm, being sent on a fool's errand by some crazy-ass queen." He rolled to his side and faced Lucero. "How did you know the connection inside the purifier was loose?"

"Caught that, hmmm?"

Ivan nodded. "Yeah, I may have been scared, but I have a near-perfect memory. I remember everything."

Lucero sighed. "Convenient in your line of work. This electrical technician thing you do."

Ivan shook his head. "Not necessarily. It's a double-edged sword. Great at work, but not so good in my personal life." Sadness crossed his face. "But I'm not here to talk about past lovers. So, spill. How did you know?"

He stared up at the ceiling. "Because, in the past, every time I've had to fix the damned purifier, the connection between the power supply and the main board caused the issue. The vegetation creeps inside and disrupts the power flow." He pushed off the floor with one foot, sending the rocker into motion. "In reality, the purifier only delays the problem tearing apart the royal clutch."

"What do you mean? Once it's running, it purifies the water. Whatever is poisoning the clutch is gone."

"That's what the queen would like you to think." He drummed his fingers on the arms of the chair. "When the king first fell sick, it took some time and a lot of testing, but I narrowed it down to microorganisms in the water. Unfortunately, it was too late for the king. He died. With the vaccine I was able to produce, I managed to treat the rest of the clutch."

Ivan toyed with the blanket under him. "Then why is the clutch sick again? Why am I, for that matter?"

Lucero sighed. "Because the organisms became resistant to my vaccines. All it took was for the purifier to fail again, and the next strain was stronger. More people fell sick. It was a vicious cycle, weakening everyone, other than me. The same nanos allowing me to analyze, process, and produce vaccines, also kill any bacteria or virus attacking my system."

"A rather handy feature." Ivan nodded. "So tell me more about these microorganisms. Are they in the water naturally?"

"Yes, but, over time, they've become mutated and more resistant from the energy the clutch uses for cooking, heating, even bathing. I advised the queen we should abandon the royal clutch, move to a place not contaminated, and rely solely on solar and other natural alternatives for energy." Anger surfaced in Lucero as memories of those who paid the consequences because of her continued stubbornness. "She refused to leave her home because of some microorganism. She was the queen, and I would eradicate the threat. And if I spoke of leaving again, she threatened to decommission me."

"Decommission? As in kill you? Isn't that drastic?"

Lucero arched a brow at him. "You've met the queen, right? What do you think?"

Ivan sighed, frustration crossing his face. "Yeah, that's what I would do. Threaten to kill the one thing who can manufacture the vaccine that saves my ass. I gave her more credit than she's due. It's obvious you came to the same conclusion and left. What happened?"

"Vihaan fell sick." The words felt like shards of glass as he pushed them past his throat. His eyes burned. "No amount of vaccine and other medicines I pushed into his body helped. The newest strain of virus was too much for his weakened system. The day after he died, I went into the forest to fix the purifier again. But the more I worked on it, the angrier I got. Because of her stupidity, I lost my lover. I couldn't go back just to start the process over again. So, instead, I fixed the purifier one last time and walked away. In the eighteen cycles I've been gone, many have searched for me, but few ventured this deep until...."

"Until the queen sent me in to unclog the purifier again." Ivan rolled onto his back, his limbs sprawled in a way so reminiscent of Vihaan, Lucero wasn't sure if he wanted to cry or jump the man. "After losing your lover, there's probably nothing I could offer to convince you to return to the royal clutch, is there?"

Lucero astonished himself when the words flew out of his mouth. "I want the *tribus noctibus*. Give me three nights of pleasure, and I will return with you."

Ivan frowned and pushed up on one arm. "What do you mean three nights of pleasure? You're *demanding* I sleep with you, in exchange for something you've done before?"

He gave a hoarse chuckle. "No, you're asking me to return to a life of watching those around me die, of being under the thumb of a queen who cares more for land than those who live on it. Well, I won't go back to that kind of hell without being compensated."

"And forcing me to have sex with you is your way of being paid? How do you even know I'm into men?"

Lucero continued to rock but met Ivan's gaze. "I'd never force you to do anything you didn't want, Ivan. I'm designed to take care of others. The same thing telling me you're approximately two-hundred-and-sixty-five pounds and six-foot-five assures me you are more than just attracted to me. When I get close, your heart rate accelerates, your breathing becomes faster, and your blood pools in your groin."

Ivan sat up with a surge of powerful muscles, his face red. "You scanned me?"

"In a fashion. The same sensors allowing me to diagnose illness pick up things like elevated heartbeat and heavy breathing." Lucero crossed his arms over his chest. "So it's simple. You find me attractive, and I've been alone a long time. You need me to go back to the clutch, and I find myself yearning for what I've been so long without—a lover. Agree to this, and I'll return to the clutch with you at the end of the three days."

"Just like that?" Suspicion colored Ivan's words.

Lucero nodded. "If you make it through all three days, Ivan. However, what I view as sexual pleasure may be more than what you're used to."

Ivan's eyes widened. "What exactly are we talking about here? You tie me up and beat me?"

A smile tugged at the corners of his mouth. "Eventually, but, I assure you the *dolore voluptatem* doesn't come until the second night, and will be quite pleasurable for both of us." Lucero stood. "What I'm asking for is your submission. Give over to me, and if you make it the entire three days, I'll have not only shown you pleasure like you've never known before, but I shall also return with you to the royal clutch." He moved to the doorway. "Outside this hall, there is a door leading to a path that will take you down to the hidden hot springs. You may safely bathe there. If you're willing, when you're done, return here in nothing but a towel."

Ivan clenched his jaw. "And if I'm not?"

Lucero ran his gaze over the man, noting everything from the thick ridge at the apex of Ivan's thighs to the tense set of his shoulders. "If not, then use my hot springs for cleansing, dress, and return here. I'll take you back to the clutch in the morning, but I will not remain. The choice is yours, Ivan." Not willing to push himself any further, Lucero left the room.

Chapter Four

Ivan paused outside the door to main room then wiped his palms on the towel wrapped around his waist. While he'd bathed in the decadence of the heated spring, it had seemed so simple. Sleeping with Lucero shouldn't be any different than sex with the robot he'd created after Jackson had left him. The cyborg had meant nothing to him. But even as his trembling fingers reached for the door handle, he knew this would be different. Having sex with the Steve 2000, as Ivan had dubbed him, wasn't the same as submitting to a machine. But what choice did he have?

After he slipped through the entry, he strode across the room, aware he wore nothing more than a length of cloth wrapped around his lean hips. As he glanced around the room for Lucero, he couldn't help but wonder if he hadn't made a mistake by agreeing to this. *What person in his right mind trades his body in exchange for something any decent human would willingly offer? Me, evidently.*

He shivered as the airflow through the room was disrupted. He was no longer alone, but he didn't turn.

Lucero. Ivan didn't know if he should be relieved or angry about it. Nor, did he trust himself to not chicken out at the last second. If he did, would Lucero force him?

He jumped when hands that should've been cold, but weren't, settled on his shoulders. The heated brush of lips across the back of his neck sent a jolt of awareness down his spine. He stifled the moan trying to break free. How had Lucero known his neck was sensitive?

"Hmm." The husky approval surprised him. "You taste better than I dared to hope."

Ivan gritted his teeth when the tormenting mouth slid down between his shoulder blades. His body responded, despite his brain's protest the man touching him wasn't real. *He's a machine.* "Don't...." He shivered when moist heat flicked over his skin, as Lucero dropped to his knees behind him. Ivan's cock hardened in a rush. It was all too easy to imagine what Lucero's tongue would do if it were on other parts of his anatomy.

"Don't what, *amans*?" Lucero moved farther down, until the hot brand of his tongue teased the base of his spine. "By returning in the towel, you agreed to this. No one is forcing you."

He hissed when Lucero nipped at his hip, just above the damp fabric. "You never said you would—"

"Would what, Ivan?" Lucero stood, his clothing brushing against Ivan's back. "Touch?" His fingers peeled away the towel. The room whirled as Ivan found himself face-to-face with the cyborg. "That I wouldn't want to explore all you have to offer?" His eyes glittered in the dim light. "From a man who's been alone too long, you should expect nothing less. I'm starving—"his thumb rubbed over Ivan's lower lip, "—for you."

Then his head dipped and the full lips he had lusted after earlier covered his own. All he could think of was how though he might have agreed to submit, he hadn't expected to respond like this. His protest died in his throat as Lucero's tongue thrust deep inside to lick at his, leaving him helpless against each flick. They tormented and beckoned, until he returned the intimate caress with every ounce of desire flooding his body. He no longer cared why this was wrong. Or why he shouldn't lose himself in the sensations the kiss created. Instead, he wanted it to never end.

A low whimper escaped him when Lucero abandoned his mouth with a rough sigh. "Delicious, just as I suspected."

"Ah...." He wasn't sure what Lucero expected him to say, if anything. His brain was scrambled to the point all he wanted was more. Had the man drugged him somehow? Had it been in the waters of the hot spring? Some miniscule organism which caused a rampant lust so fierce it lowered what little inhibition Ivan possessed?

"Shhh...." Lucero placed a fingertip over his lips. "For this night only, you shall focus on the *tactus*."

"*Tactus*?" Ivan sounded like a parrot, but was unable to stop himself.

"It's a ritual of sorts." Lucero's amber eyes now resembled molten gold. "The night of the touch has been a sacred rite of the Krontos people for eons. It's used as a gateway to our mating." His fingers left Ivan's lips to trace over his chin then continued down his neck to his shoulder. "It allows a couple to explore each other without committing to one another."

"Explore?" Ivan croaked, while a shiver wracked his frame as the light touch grazed one of his nipples.

"Yes. With our fingers...." He plucked at the hard flesh he'd been teasing.

Ivan hissed as the slight sting pooled in his groin.

"With our lips...." Lucero wrapped an arm around his waist and lifted Ivan with ease. It had to be

Lucero's cyborg strength, but Ivan didn't have time to contemplate the feat. Lucero's mouth brushed over the swell of his chest.

"Ah, shit...." He buried his hands in Lucero's hair as the other man nuzzled his chest.

"And, of course," a low rumble escaped Lucero, "our tongues."

Ivan whimpered as wet heat washed over his skin before it curled around his nipple. A plea trembled on his lips when Lucero pulled back.

"In my culture, once a couple has joined during the final rite, they've become as one. Perfect mates in every sense until the day we die." He kept his gaze on Ivan as he lowered him back to the floor. "They will no longer desire others, but only one another." He chuckled. "When Vihaan died, a part of me did as well. Your presence has resurrected it."

Ivan swallowed hard. "And you want this with me?" His mind whirled. "I agreed to three nights of pleasure, not some mating ritual." He drew a deep breath. "I don't do permanent, ever. And not with a man who is probably more machine than not."

"Relax, Ivan. Mated for life isn't always the result." Lucero crossed his arms over his chest. "Now, close your eyes."

A fissure of fear tried to combat the desire the command drew forth. "Why?"

A slow, seductive smile crossed Lucero's face. "Because, one way or another, tonight you will realize I am a man, albeit enhanced. But I breathe, I bleed. I feel just as keenly as any other."

Dread built inside Ivan's stomach and only became worse when a slender piece of woven cloth appeared in the cyborg's hands. "What do you plan to do with that?"

Lucero pulled it through his fingers, looping it around in a fashion almost mesmerizing. "There are many senses one possesses. Touch, smell, taste, and even hearing, but none quite as potent as our vision." He slipped the cloth over Ivan's head. "Perhaps, without your sight, you'll finally be able to see."

Taking a step back, Lucero stared at the naked man in front of him. Every ion of his being, both mechanical and *Siserian*, wanted to see if it was even possible to claim Ivan. From his cropped midnight hair to his strong feet, he was a banquet to Lucero's enhanced senses. Layered muscles over a sturdy frame, wide shoulders tapering to narrow hips tempted him. He wanted to partake, to immerse himself in the man in front of him. But he couldn't rush this. There had to be order. His very soul demanded it. The other man might not understand the importance of *tactus*, or the stark need driving Lucero, but the mating urge coursed through him with every ounce of air he brought into his lungs.

"You're a very attractive man, Ivan, but I'm sure you've been told that before." He circled him. "But it makes me wonder, is what's inside as attractive?"

Ivan followed the sound of Lucero's voice. "Does it matter?"

Lucero paused. "Of course it matters." He stroked his hand down Ivan's spine and loved the way the man jumped. "Too often we place too much emphasis on our outward appearances." Leaning forward, he was tempted to bury his nose in the damp curls at the base of his neck, but instead settled for blowing against the damp flesh. A smile tugged at his lips when goose bumps prickled Ivan's skin. His Ivan was more sensitive than he'd ever dreamed. The possibilities for tomorrow's tests teased him, but he forced them to the wayside. He needed to guide his Ivan through the first test, before he could even think of what pleasures awaited during the *dolore voluptatem*.

Instead he pressed a kiss between Ivan's shoulder blades and allowed just the tip of his tongue to brush over his back before retreating.

"Lucero...please." A ragged plea.

"Oh, believe me, I intend to, once you give yourself over to me." He placed his hands on slender hips then savored the warmth of the skin under his fingertips. "I promise nothing bad will occur." He emphasized the point by raking his nails over raised pelvic bones.

A rattling sigh escaped Ivan. "You ask for more than pleasure."

"Mmmm," he agreed as his lips traced over Ivan's collarbone. "Of course, but it all starts with pleasure." Nipping the warm skin, he trailed his right hand up Ivan's side to map out every inch of his lover's ribs until Ivan trapped his wandering digits between his bulging bicep and muscular pec. Ivan's chuckle made him smile as he explored the thick chest in front of him. The idea such a large man might be ticklish amused him. What other contradictory things would he find during their three nights? He didn't know, but he was eager to find out.

"Release me, Ivan." He kept his voice low but firm as he paused, his mouth mere inches from a pebbled nipple. The other man's submission to him was given. There could be no other outcome.

A puff of air passed Ivan's lips, but he obeyed and relaxed his arm.

"Good boy." He laved the flesh just to the side of Ivan's sternum then traced a figure-eight pattern, his tongue grazing the edge of the hardened peak. Above his head, Ivan hissed.

"I'm no boy." The protest was hoarse, a tremor shaking his frame.

Against his stomach, the hard ridge of Ivan's cock teased Lucero. His left hand abandoned Ivan's hipbone to wrap around the erection, his thumb rubbing over the fluid weeping from the flared head. He cursed, and Lucero smiled. "You're no boy with a weapon like this between your thighs." He tightened his grip. "But, make no mistake, you'll be my boy before we leave." Giving the captured flesh short, firm strokes, he straightened and took in the tight planes of Ivan's face as he varied his rhythm.

"Son of a bitch." Ivan's head dropped back to expose the long, tanned column of his throat. "Your hands." He bit his lower lip, his blindfolded eyes making the action even more arousing to Lucero. He could only imagine what went on inside his lover's head. The thrill of controlling the other man's pleasure was heady and one he hadn't felt in so long.

"Are what? Talented?" Lucero's hand slowed. "They should be. I've spent plenty of time masturbating in the two years since I left the clutch."

"It shows." Ivan bucked toward him, his hips jerking toward Lucero's touch. "Fuck, more." A bead of sweat rolled down his jaw.

"Like this?" Lucero whispered. His eyes drifted down to the thick *gallus* he held. Raised veins decorated the underside, and the flared head was almost crimson. A thick sac peppered with dark curls hung under the curved stalk. But the contrast between his dark hand and the pale flesh had him panting. He'd never seen anything so erotic. Ivan wasn't ruddy like Vihaan had been. No, the off-worlder's flesh was an almost translucent milk white. It was as if Ivan's groin had been marked by the moon. The phenomenon was riveting. "You are so light here."

"Tan line," Ivan gritted out between clenched teeth. "From my swim trunks."

Lucero paused. "I do not know of this tan line, but I find it very"—he released Ivan with the intentions of guiding the man to the pallet—"tempting."

An almost brutal sound tore from Ivan's chest, his cock bouncing back up to slap against his pebbled abs. His arm flexed when he reached between their bodies. "Fuck."

Lucero intercepted his hand. "No."

Ivan's nostrils flared. "What do you mean 'no'?"

"I will be the *only* one to give you pleasure." He tugged Ivan forward then changed his mind about their destination. He needed to see the man sprawled out on his bed. "But, first, we will be more comfortable."

Why he let the cyborg lead him around, Ivan didn't know. Well, he did. It all had to do with the increasing ache in his balls. When he'd chosen to submit, he hadn't expected much more than an order to bend over. Instead, Lucero had surprised him by exploring his body. With very little effort he'd pushed Ivan to his very limits. Which also surprised him. He was used to immediate release. In the past, he'd orgasmed when he wanted.

Hell, he'd controlled every second of his past intimate encounters. His lovers had enjoyed his dominant personality in the bedroom, but it eventually became a bone of contention when he wanted the same in return. *Especially with Jackson.* He'd been fine with Ivan ordering him around, but had struggled with the idea of even raising his voice in return. Which is why it had hurt so much when he had come home to find his lover and all of Jackson's belongings gone. He'd decided then he'd never find a man he could submit to, because it was nothing more than a fantasy. *One better left alone.*

As he tripped over what felt like a door jamb, he pulled himself out of his morbid thoughts and focused on the here and now. "Where are you taking me?"

"To my sleeping chambers." Lucero took him by the shoulders, guiding Ivan until the edge of something touched the back of his knees. He gave a grunt when the other man tumbled him onto a soft, thick mattress. Then Lucero was over him, the heat of his body pressed against his. Without his sight, every inch of his skin felt electrified where it rubbed against the coarse fabric of Lucero's clothing. Would the man ever get naked?

"I think one of us is seriously overdressed." He'd wanted flirty, but his words came out more like a growl.

"Patience." Strong fingers skimmed up the undersides of his arms then urged them above Ivan's head. "There are bars on the headboard just above you. I want you to hang onto them, Ivan."

With trembling fingers, Ivan felt around for the bars until Lucero guided his hands to where he wanted them. The satin-smooth wood teased his palms as he obeyed.

"Good." Lucero drew back with a sharp inhalation. "Damned if you're not tempting my control, off-worlder."

Ghost-like caresses skimmed along his abs, avoided his aching cock, to settle on the sensitive flesh of his inner thighs.

"So, here's the deal, the moment you let go, this all stops. But while your hands remain where they are, I will give you pleasure like none you've ever known." A thread of steel infused Lucero's voice. "Do you understand?"

He nodded, his hips lifting off the bedding when Lucero's calloused fingers found his scrotum. "Hands on, you continue, hands off, you stop." He gritted his teeth as the cyborg cupped his tight balls in his palm. "I got it."

A low chuckle reached his ears. "Actually, I think I'm the one who has it."

A gentle pressure tightened around his gonads. Ivan bit his lip to keep his moan to himself. He loved having his balls played with, the rougher the better, but damned if he'd tell him so.

The grip loosened, and Ivan wanted to beg for the return of the harder touch. "Hiding your pleasure won't be tolerated. You agreed to give it to me, and I'm holding you to your word."

"Fuck." Ivan pressed his head back, his hips rocking back and forth. "I need—"

"This?" Lucero's voice was closer than before, but the deft hand clamping down on him had the tortured sound escaping Ivan's tight throat. The perfect blend of pain and pleasure was as foreign as the new world he found himself in. He wanted—no, needed—to spill. Now.

"Gods, yes. Stroke me, please!" He continued to cling to the posts, his mind nothing more than a haze of pleasure, wetness enveloping the crest of his cock. "Aw, hell, I need...." His hands loosened, his need to thread them through Lucero's hair, to hold him in place until he shot down his lover's throat growing. But the second his grip slipped, the heat was gone.

"Are we stopping?" Lucero's question sent a flurry of panic through him.

"No!" He returned to his former position, but found his desire to touch the man between his thighs grew with the return of Lucero's tongue. "Tie them!"

"No." The graze of lips against the crease of his thigh tormented him, but reminded him of who was in charge. "They will remain untied. Your submission, your pleasure must be freely given. It's not something I will take."

"Shit." Tears pricked at his covered eyes. "I can't promise I won't slip. The pleasure, the pain...is too much." A huge sigh shook his body. "But damned if I don't want it."

"Then you will endure and remember my command. Let go and this is over. I will send you back to the great room, unfulfilled."

"I get it." He squeezed the wood until he was sure his knuckles were white with the effort.

"That's my boy."

Before Ivan could grumble about the claim, he was shot right back to the edge of sanity as Lucero rolled his balls while sucking him deep inside of his mouth. Ivan's breath caught then released on almost a wail. The sensations of warm lips tugging on his glans while the touch of strong fingers against his hair-roughened sac piled upon one another until the ominous crack of

71

wood above his head echoed through the room. Desperate to come, he stilled, afraid he'd break the spindles free, and Lucero would abandon him. He groaned as Lucero released his cock, his tongue tracing down the underside to lash at the base.

"So close, but can you give over?" Lucero sounded hoarse. "Will you submit?"

"I"—he tried to focus—"I need to come."

A low hum tickled his balls before dipping below them. He almost shouted when wet heat bathed his asshole. His butt flexed, whether to trap Lucero inside or force him out, he didn't know.

"Mmmmm." The vibration radiated through his groin as Lucero gave him one slow tug from base to tip. Tension boiled over in his stomach as his release approached. He shot hard just as Lucero's thumb found the sensitive spot just below the head. Ivan screamed as his body convulsed then tried to turn itself inside out as his seed flowed out of him in several hard surges.

As he finished, he could barely make sense of the words Lucero whispered against his ear, as he unwrapped Ivan's hands. "Good boy...."

Euphoria embraced him as the warmth of Lucero's still-clothed body settled over him. Tired, but relaxed from his release, he tumbled into the dark abyss of slumber.

Chapter Five

Ivan jerked awake when the scent of food hit his nostrils. Sitting up, he let the sheet pool around his waist. A thin pallet cushioned the floor. Around him, sunshine poured in the curtainless windows. Memories of the night before crashed over him, the undeniable pleasure of his submission to a man who wasn't really a man then the sullen silence from the cyborg when he'd staggered from the bed.

"Where are you going?"

Ivan ripped away the blindfold and rolled into a sitting position to see Lucero frown, puzzlement stamped all over his face.

"Back out to the living room." He pushed off the mattress then swayed on his feet, his knees weaker than he'd expected. The urge to flee rode him hard. Nothing could ever compare to what had just happened. He'd thought he'd been an experienced

lover, but a cyborg had just shown him how little he knew about pleasure and submission.

"Why?" The question came out flat.

"Don't take it personally, but I don't sleep with anyone. It's a trust thing." He glanced over his shoulder to see the man sprawled across the rumpled linens. His raven curls were damp with sweat, his shirt clung to his torso, and, dear Lord, the thick erection pressed against the front of his pants made Ivan's mouth water. Lost to his own pleasure, he hadn't noticed the cyborg hadn't taken his own. "Shit. You didn't come." He twisted at the waist in an effort to sit down on the edge of the bed, but instead landed in an indelicate heap next to Lucero.

"No, I didn't." The words seemed brittle, but when Ivan sat up and reached for the button on Lucero's pants, the other man wrapped his hand around Ivan's wrist. "And I won't tonight."

He gaped at Lucero in disbelief. "What do you mean, you won't?" He prided himself in satisfying his partners. The thought of leaving the other man in such a state bothered him. Unless the cyborg didn't orgasm like a normal man?

His thoughts must've been obvious because Lucero snarled. "Don't look at me like that. I can come, but I refuse to gift my pleasure to a man who will not even sleep in my arms. So unless you've changed your mind about where you're sleeping tonight, there won't be any release for me."

Ivan chewed on his lower lip then jerked his wrist free. "That's blackmail. This is about sex, not intimacy. I never expected you to not take your own pleasure. In fact, it was part of our bargain."

Lucero shook his head. "If you believe that, you're a bigger fool than I thought. We agreed to three nights of pleasure. I never specified who would experience it. You've had yours, so your obligation for tonight is done."

"But that's not fair!" Ivan ran his hand through his hair. "You can't expect me to leave you like that." He nodded toward Lucero's groin.

"You're not." Lucero folded his arms over his chest. "I'm telling you to go."

"But you're hard. It's gotta be uncomfortable...." He struggled to wrap his brain around the fact Lucero refused to allow Ivan to touch. "Why?"

Lucero sighed. "Every man has limits. Just as you refuse to sleep with me, I won't allow you to pleasure me then run away. I have more respect for myself." Then he rolled over, his back stiff. "When you go through the door, walk down the shorter of the two halls. The living room is on your left."

For a long time Ivan stared at Lucero's tense frame, shame riding him hard. He had not meant to hurt him with his refusal. It just irked Ivan he wasn't allowed to give the cyborg the same pleasure. But he had no one to blame but himself. His own stupidity sometimes astonished him.

"Look, I'm sorry if I implied...."

"Just go, Ivan. It's been a very long night. I was injured when I fought the morte'metentis *and I'm tired. Even machines need to sleep."*

A fresh flood of shame washed over him. The truth stung, and with his turned back it was obvious the cyborg had dismissed him. He mumbled another sorry before slipping out of the room.

Now with the bright sunshine around him, he would have to face Lucero over breakfast and pray the cyborg would allow him to continue the tests. While he still held a glimmer of hope about his return home, his curiosity about the second test was stronger. Would Lucero do more than touch him this time? Would he fuck him? His need for more shocked him. He should be pissed at the position Lucero had put him in. He should be demanding the cyborg take him back to the royal clutch, not anticipating the next time he submitted to the other man. But a small part of him would hate himself forever if he didn't at least explore the opportunity.

"Are you planning to lounge around all day, or are you hungry?" Lucero appeared in the entryway of the kitchen, a hand towel tossed over one wide shoulder. The dark-tan shirt he wore unbuttoned exposed an expanse of skin Ivan wanted to touch. "If so, breakfast is on the table."

"Yeah, I'm coming." He flushed when Lucero's eyes darkened before the cyborg disappeared back into the kitchen.

Lucero drew a deep breath as he braced his palms on the counter. The desperate hunger in Ivan's gaze had almost brought him to his knees, along with starting an internal war within him he wasn't sure he would win. His need to give pleasure, to have a lover at his mercy, was stronger than it ever had been. Even Vihaan's submission hadn't rocked him this close to his core. He wanted to give Ivan every drop of dominance he had. To show the off-worlder he would never find what Lucero offered in another's arms. He shouldn't be feeling this way about a man who wanted to use him as a means to return home, but he did. Lucero called himself all kinds of an idiot. Ivan could come to the table and tell him he didn't wish to finish the tests, that Lucero had pushed too hard last night.

Too hard?

A soft chuckle escaped him at the thought. If Ivan only knew. The submission he'd required last night would be small compared to what he'd demand tonight, if Ivan chose to stay. He'd not only tie the man to his bed, but put Ivan's submissiveness to the test with not only his body, but with the best Sisera had to offer. Would Ivan pass? A shadow of doubt filled him. Only time would tell, and perhaps, in the end, it would be better if he did take the off-worlder back to the royal clutch before the connection he'd experienced last night grew any stronger. Before he became more invested. But now the three nights had begun, how could he let the man go?

"Damn, it smells good in here."

Ivan's voice so close behind him startled Lucero, and he jerked, clenching his fingers around the lip of the counter. "Thanks. Go ahead and help yourself. I'm just getting the cups for our juice." Shaking off his growing discomfort, he reached above his head to pull out two clean wooden cups. "I made it fresh this morning from the fruit of the *veneno* and collected rainwater from last night's storm."

When he pivoted to face the table, he found Ivan already seated, dishing up steaming food onto both plates. As if sensing his stare, Ivan paused and glanced up, before continuing.

"It stormed last night? I didn't hear anything."

Carrying the cups and the glass pitcher of juice, he made his way over to the off-worlder. "It was late, after you were asleep. It usually rains in the wee hours of the morning. I have several collection units outside to catch fresh water for drinking." He placed his burden on the table and settled in the chair across from Ivan. "While the hot spring is good for bathing and cleansing, I don't care for the taste of the water."

"Salty?" Ivan shifted in his chair then poured a cup of the juice.

Lucero shook his head, wondering why they were discussing water of all things. "No. It has to do with the minerals in the springs. There is a faint taste of metal. It isn't harmful if digested. I just don't care for the taste of it."

Ivan nodded. "Gotcha." He picked up his utensil and began to eat.

Picking at his own breakfast, Lucero stewed over how to handle the ever-building tension. One of them would eventually have to talk about what had happened last night. But before they did, he had to decide on a course of action. If Ivan wanted to return to the royal clutch, they'd have to leave soon, or he'd risk traversing the An'tealan Forest after dark on his return trip. *But what if he wants to stay?* The thought sent a surge of blood heading south. The possibility of having another night with the sexy man under his control tore at Lucero's patience.

"Staring at the food isn't going to get it into your body." Ivan leaned back in his chair. "Or is my company so unpleasant you've lost your appetite?"

"No." He pushed his unfinished meal away and braced his elbows on the table. "Do you want me to take you back to the clutch today?"

Ivan's hand, which had been lifting the cup to his mouth, froze midair. Something undefinable swam in the depths of his eyes, before he masked it. "I thought our agreement was for three days."

"It was." Lucero shrugged. "However, you have the choice of backing out. I'll still return you to the clutch."

Carefully lowering the cup to the table, Ivan licked his lower lip. Lucero couldn't help but stare at the shiny surface, but kept reminding himself they needed this discussion before he could act upon his urges.

"But you won't stay, correct?"

Lucero nodded. "I haven't hidden my lack of desire to return, off-worlder. Short of three nights of pleasure, nothing will convince me."

Ivan contemplated him for several long moments before pushing away from the table. His tone was gruff and there was a discernable bulge at the juncture of his thighs. "Then I guess you're stuck with me for another night."

Even as tempted as he was to take Ivan's answer at face value, his sense of fair play told him he needed to give the other man one final out. "Even if what I required of you last night is child's play compared to what I will demand tonight?"

Other than clenching his jaw and the slight flare of his nose, Ivan met his eyes with little emotion. "Of course. I wish to go home, and I honor my promises."

Ignoring the sting from Ivan's words, Lucero rose and gathered up his dishes. "As you wish." He turned toward the sink. "I have several tasks I need to complete today. I suggest you rest for tonight."

"You think you're going to wear me out?" Ivan set his empty plate down next to Lucero. "You'll find I have more stamina than the average man."

Lucero peeked at him through his lashes. "I don't doubt it in the least. However, you've never experienced the *dolore voluptatem*. It can tax the control of even the strongest of men."

A flicker of something crossed Ivan's face then he pursed his lips. "Planning on hurting me, cyborg?"

Unable to resist the challenge in his tone, Lucero pivoted, thrust his fingers into Ivan's hair, and jerked his head down all in one smooth move. "Only in the most pleasurable way possible." Then he covered the man's slack mouth with his. After bestowing a brutal kiss that had his cock aching, he pulled back, spun Ivan around by the shoulders, and gave him a gentle shove toward the living room. "When the bell on the mantle chimes five, go to the hot spring and bathe thoroughly, but refrain from release. I want you in my bedroom, clean and aroused, by the time it chimes eight."

***

After exploring the house in Lucero's absence, Ivan returned to the living room. Now, lounging on his pallet, he gazed out the window. He'd given up counting the birds flying past the opening. They were just too frequent, but it probably wouldn't have mattered if they'd been dive-bombing the house. Little could distract him from what would happen tonight. It was the unknown. What exactly did Lucero have planned for him? And would he enjoy it?

Across the room, the bell chimed. He kept his gaze on the window. The randomness of the clock was odd. Instead of being chronological as he'd expected, the clock seemed to skip around. One hour it would chime three times then the next seven. But that didn't stop Ivan's breath catching each time it rang.

One.

He gritted his teeth, his frustration all consuming. He was ready to bathe.

Two.

Gathering up the blanket under him, he fisted the material. He wanted to prepare himself.

Three.

He gasped, his cock tenting his pants at the idea of cleaning every inch of his body for Lucero. The urge to please the other man consumed him.

Four.

He jerked upright. The need for Lucero's dominance shook him. *Dear Lord, please.*

Five.

"Finally." He scrambled to his feet and fled the room, heading toward the waiting hot spring.

It took less than two minutes for him to follow the hallway and slip through the doorway and down the gradual slope leading to his destination. At the bottom, the path gave way to lush forest and the hot spring surrounded by dense vegetation and steam. Pulling his clothing off, he hung his shirt and pants over a low-hanging branch and slipped into the steamy water. He groaned as warm water engulfed first his feet then his calves before rising up to lap at his thighs. A low hiss passed his lips as he sank down onto the natural stone shelf, liquid heat enveloping his hips, ass, and groin. The smooth ledge at the shallower end made the perfect seat. His erection bobbed obscenely in front of him, just under the surface, but he chose to ignore it as he leaned his head back against the smooth rock lip.

The natural jetties of water caressed every inch of his body, teasing him with what pleasure could be had. He counted to a hundred in his head, but even that didn't help. It only stroked his desire higher.

Desperate, he reached down and cupped his shaft, tightening his fingers until his lower body trembled. He bit his lower lip, hoping the pain would distract him, but, if anything, it sent the hunger soaring higher. Dare he disobey?

Lucero kept to the shadows just beyond the hot spring. His gaze never wavered as he skirted the far edge of the clearing. From his vantage point, he could see the wide outline of Ivan's shoulders and heavily-muscled back. The wispy steam wrapped around the off-worlder, tempting Lucero unbearably. He wanted to join the man. To run his hands over the broad planes of Ivan's chest, to follow the dark trail of hair down to the impressive cock the water hid. But he wasn't supposed to be here, playing the voyeur. He'd left this morning with the best intentions of gathering everything he needed for tonight. He'd spent the time wisely, collecting the *ardentem,* a self-heating oil, and harvesting a rather nice specimen of *aculeatum herba,* a tuberous root he couldn't wait to use on Ivan. Added to the flogger he'd woven out of *tuerentur fronds* after his midday meal, he was well prepared for the evening. Then a quick check of his traps had led him close to his home. And to the temptation within.

Shifting the heavy bag slung crosswise over his chest, Lucero slipped closer when Ivan gave a muffled moan. Had the other man hurt himself or slipped on the not-so-smooth bottom of the hot spring? His concern for his guest changed when Ivan's shoulders jerked then rocked forward. His suspicions aroused, he adjusted his position to one where he could see into the pool. He barely managed to stifle his growl when the mist parted and he caught a glimpse of Ivan's hand moving over his erection. Lust pooled in his stomach. He clutched a nearby branch to keep from interrupting. Every instinct he possessed screamed at him to make his presence known, to rip Ivan's hand away then bend the stubborn man over his knee and show him the error of his ways. That orgasm was *his*.

"Fuck, I need to come." The whispered words floated to Lucero's sensitive ears as the water sloshed faster. He took a step back when Ivan surged to his feet, his hand digging into the rocky edge of the pool, his thick cock smacking his abs. "God damn, I'm pathetic. Can't even get off without permission."

Ivan's obvious frustration should've pleased him, but instead the desire to slip into the water and give him the release he desired was stronger than Lucero expected. He wanted to reassure the off-worlder what he felt was only natural. Ivan's need to obey his orders wasn't pathetic, nor was his need to submit. But now wasn't the time. During the height of the *dolore voluptatem* he would make sure the man understood—even if he had to be cruel about it.

As Ivan rubbed the soap over his body in broad sweeping motions, Lucero backed farther into the shadows, leaving his guest to his bath. All too soon, he'd have Ivan at his mercy, tied to his bed. The other man had agreed to it.

Chapter Six

Ivan winced as a rough stone dug into his heel. He paused and lifted his foot to examine the sole. Finished with his bath, he now stood in the middle of the path with a towel wrapped around his waist. Squinting against the dying light, he brushed the debris away. He couldn't see anything, but damned if it didn't sting. He let his foot drop back down then cursed as the towel unknotted and fell to the ground. "Son of a bitch." He'd bent to retrieve it, when a hand found his back. He jumped, but a familiar voice teased his ear.

"Leave it." Lucero's hand slid down to tease his ass.

He squeezed his eyes shut, torn between the need to push back against the fingers exploring his crease and pulling away from the all-too-intimate touch. The brush of Lucero's clothed body against his behind him had him swaying forward. He'd have fallen flat on his face, if it hadn't been for the firm grip the cyborg had on him.

"Lucero." The name emerged a plea when the wet wash of a tongue against the inner curves of his ass registered. Was the other man actually licking his ass?

He squirmed and panted, his cock filling fast. He twisted hard when Lucero sighed then flicked at his rosette, wetting the surface before tapping it. "Shit...."

"Stop. Be still." The dark, forceful order left no room for disobedience. Nor did the strong hand which grasped the base of Ivan's dick.

He groaned. If someone had told him six months ago he'd be in an alien realm, willingly allowing a cyborg to lick his ass while he submitted to him, he'd have asked what the fool was smoking. But now all he could do was obey while Lucero nuzzled his sac.

"You taste wonderful. Clean with a hint of musk. Just like a man should." He sighed, his breath teasing the sensitive flesh, causing goose bumps to run down Ivan's legs. "It's almost enough to make me forget about the *dolore voluptatem* and take you right here."

Ivan panted, his eyes squeezed shut. "Hell, yeah." Aroused and more than ready for release, he didn't care if Lucero fucked him in full view at Grand Central Station.

A low grumble and Lucero's sudden abandonment of his ass quashed his hopes. "Lucky for you, I have more self-control. I wish I could say the same for you." Lucero nipped his shoulder, pulling Ivan upright. "You cheated, *amans*."

"What?" He gritted his teeth when Lucero tugged hard on his cock.

"In the hot spring...you pleasured yourself." Lucero scattered kisses across his shoulders between each word.

Trying to concentrate on the reprimand, Ivan shivered under the damp touch of the cyborg's mouth. "I didn't come."

"But not for a lack of trying." Lucero swatted him, his hand landing hard against Ivan's left butt cheek.

Ivan groaned then swayed forward. Pained pleasure raced from his ass to his cock, causing him to swell even more.

"Hmmm." Lucero's rumble of approval was followed by a slow, long lap of his tongue up the side of Ivan's neck. "Someone likes a bite of pain with his pleasure." He nuzzled Ivan's ear. "Good thing because tonight is all about pleasured pain."

"Shit." Even he could hear the longing in his voice. He stumbled when Lucero gave him a firm push forward, guiding him up the path, naked. "What about my towel?"

"Leave it. I have better things to do than unwrap you tonight. Besides you wouldn't have worn it long, anyway." Lucero followed him up the gradual incline.

When they reached the doorway which led into the house, Ivan swallowed hard, uncertainty suddenly striking him. Was he ready for this? His cock screamed yes, but the part that had never recovered from Jackson's desertion wasn't so sure.

As if in tune to his needs, Lucero placed a comforting hand on his hip. "Second thoughts?"

Ivan shuddered under his palm. "Kind of."

There was a long pause behind him, and if Ivan expected the other man to back off and give him a gentle out, he was mistaken.

"Talk to me."

The request surprised Ivan. "You want to talk, now?" A slight breeze filtered up the pathway and washed over his bare skin. He shivered.

"Yes." There was no give in the cyborg's tone. "I will not force you, but neither will I let you back out because you're scared."

Ivan opened his mouth to protest. A grown man didn't get scared. He was strong, determined, and above all else, fearless. Or so he kept telling himself.

"Don't. Only a fool would deny what he fears." Lucero used his grip to turn Ivan then pressed up against him, trapping him between his fully-clothed body and the door. "What about tonight bothers you?

The lack of control? I can assure you, I won't let any permanent harm fall upon you. I'll push you to your limits and a bit beyond, but my goal isn't to damage you in any way a few hours in the hot spring won't cure."

Ivan's mind whirled at the words. The endless possibilities Lucero could inflict upon him flashed before him. Spankings. Fisting. Blow Jobs. Orgasm denial. He shook at the last one. The very idea of not coming was repugnant. He craved a repeat of the release Lucero gave him like a drug addict needing his next hit.

"Ivan." Lucero's fingers moving over his cheek caught his attention. "Look at me." This close to his beautiful amber eyes, Ivan found himself tongue-tied. How could he tell a cyborg, a man half-human, half-machine, he needed the release Lucero offered? He couldn't.

"You need to talk to me." Lucero cupped his cheek, his gaze searching Ivan's. "Are you worried I'm going to physically hurt you?"

He shook his head. "At least not in a way I can't handle."

"Good. Before we make it into my room, you will pick out a word. Something to stop everything."

93

Familiar with BDSM tenets, Ivan sighed. Both he and Jackson had picked one when they'd begun playing around on the fringes of the lifestyle. "A safeword. I have one. Dahlia."

A frown furrowed Lucero's brow. "You've used one in the past? Another man has hurt you to the point you needed to call a stop?"

"No." He chewed on his lower lip, debating how much to tell Lucero. "Let's just say a previous lover and I played at a power exchange, but it didn't work out. We both had safewords. He used his once, but I never did."

Confusion crossed Lucero's face. "Explain."

Ivan flushed then averted his eyes. "I wanted him to do things to me. Things Jackson didn't feel comfortable with. In the end, he used his safeword, rather than do them."

"Ah. And these things would've brought you pleasure?"

Ivan shrugged. "Maybe, I don't know. I thought so at the time."

Lucero placed a finger under his chin and lifted Ivan's head. "What did you want him to do?"

More blood rushed to Ivan's face. "Ah, hell." He tried to pull away but was unable to free himself from Lucero's grip.

"Tell me." The order left no room for denial.

He cursed softly when Lucero stood firm. "Fuck. I wanted him to take control. Do whatever he wanted with me. Spank me, fuck me, I didn't care, just so long as he was the one calling the shots. I wanted to feel what he did when we made love."

A slow smile tugged at Lucero's lips when he cupped the back of Ivan's neck. "You want to be dominated." The wealth of pleasure in the words sent a flurry of lust to the pit of Ivan's stomach. Lucero pulled him closer. "You need me to take control, to push you past your limits until all you can do is feel?"

Ivan moaned low in his throat, his cock twitching as he clung to the shorter man. He didn't stop to question why he trusted Lucero to be able to hold him. "Yes."

"Then open the door, *amans*. I will give you what you need like your next breath."

The foreign endearment stroked over Ivan and had him fumbling behind him, until Lucero gently spun him around to face the door. His palms sweating, he wrapped his fingers around the latch. Twisting it, he pushed the door open and took a hesitant step inside.

"Keep going." Lucero encouraged. The clock on the mantel began to chime. Each strike of the bell, struck a chord deep inside of him, until the eighth ring faded away. "It's time, Ivan."

He nodded and the sudden relief of pressure flooded his veins. He straightened his shoulders then strode down the hall toward Lucero's bedroom. The cyborg would take care of him. He wouldn't fail Ivan, like Jackson had.

***

Lucero laid his toys out on the stand next to his bed as Ivan shifted against the bedding. Sprawled out like a feast fit for a king, with his arms secured to the headboard and his thick thighs tied far enough apart for Lucero to move, Ivan's body glistened in the faint candlelight. Just seeing Ivan naked and at his mercy made his dick hard. Tonight would not be the night he claimed Ivan, but he would make the man wish he had.

"Lucero?" Ivan licked his lips, his blue eyes seeking his.

"Yes?" He sat down next to him and brushed a lock of Ivan's hair back.

"Do I have to call you Master?"

Lucero tried to judge if Ivan found the idea abhorrent or not. He cocked his head. "Call me what you want. If it's Master, fine. If not, Lucero will do." He leaned down and traced his tongue over the seam of Ivan's lips. "I don't care what comes from this sexy mouth." He pulled back and gave a mock scowl. "Unless of course it's to call me by that damned scientific name and number. That will earn you an ass warming you won't forget, understand?" He squeezed Ivan's hip for emphasis.

"Yes, sir." Ivan squirmed, longing etched across his face.

"Good." Twisting at the waist, he snagged the squat jar he'd put the *ardentem* in. "Much like the *tactus,* the *dolore voluptatem* is a sacred part of our mating ritual. Tonight, I will use a variety of things, each designed to create a different sensation, to show you the way of what we call *pleasured pain.*" He unscrewed the jar, setting the lid aside. The scent of citrus filled the air. Dipping his index finger into the cool substance, he coated it then pulled it free. "This particular oil comes from the *ardentem* plant. It is rather cool when applied." Lucero drew a long line across the top of Ivan's chest. "But it has a remarkable ability to change under the right conditions." Leaning in, he breathed on the smear.

"Holy shit!" Ivan tossed his head back, the muscles in his arms flexing as he jerked on the cords binding him to the bed. "It burns."

Lucero smiled at the bound man's reaction. "Indeed, it does." He wet his finger again, this time coating Ivan's nearest nipple. "And it feels even better against more sensitive flesh."

"No, oh my god." Ivan babbled as Lucero tipped his head and blew on the distended peak. Not satisfied with a mere single plea to Ivan's god, Lucero began to paint random designs across his lover's torso. A swirly line between his pectorals, another circle around his right nipple, a sharp diagonal across each hip bone, even a heart around the man's tempting navel. But no matter what he drew, Lucero followed each mark with his warm breath.

When he bent over the heart, Ivan thrashed against the bedding, tortured sounds of pleasure spilling from his lips. Lucero took the cue to push a little harder, a little further. Plunging back inside the jar, he scooped up a large dollop of oil. "Ivan." Then he straightened, holding his fingers out. "Look at me."

The off-worlder lifted his head from the pillow, his eyes desperate, chest heaving. A low groan ripped free of him, followed by a protest. "No, more, dear lord, no more."

Studying the fast pulse, rapid breathing, and solid erection, Lucero decided his guest could handle more than he thought. "Are you safewording?"

Ivan shook his head. "No, sir."

"Then you will take more." He leaned back. "Watch." He waited until he felt Ivan's gaze upon him then smeared the oil down the underside of Ivan's cock.

"Fuck!" If it hadn't been for Lucero's restraining arm across his hipbones, Ivan would've bucked him straight off the bed, when he blew on the distended shaft. Ivan writhed against his hold, cursing him the entire time. "You rotten son of a bitch."

Lucero blew a little harder on the throbbing flesh, tightening his hand around the base.

"Ah, it fucking burns." Ivan gasped and struggled for air, his chest heaving.

"Of course, it does." Lucero gave a sharp inhale, when a spurt of liquid seeped from Ivan's domed head then ran down the stalk. He couldn't resist. He extended his tongue and caught the drop.

Ivan tried to sit up, but the cords held him securely. "Oh my god. I'm going to come."

"No, you won't." Lucero growled as he captured every drop of the pre-cum slipping free. "Your release is mine." He tightened his grip. "You don't come until I say you can. I'm in charge. Remember?"

Ivan collapsed back to the bed then whimpered deep in his throat. "Yes."

Keeping his hand around Ivan's cock, he crawled to his knees and snagged the *aculeatum herba* with his free hand. "Ready for the next step?" He posed the question more as a warning, than with any expectation of an answer.

"I guess." Ivan panted. His legs trembled against Lucero's thighs as Lucero released his cock, needing both hands for his next task. Ivan took several deep breaths, his eyes drifting shut. Lucero scowled.

"Open your eyes. I won't tell you again, *amans*. I want you to see everything I do." After Ivan's lashes fluttered then lifted, Lucero held up the *aculeatum herba*. "This is a root native to Sisera. In its natural form it has many medicinal properties." Snagging the knife off the stand, Lucero began to strip the outer skin from the lower two thirds. "While I've used it many times to help heal cuts, I've found even a better use for it since I've been on my own."

"You have?" Ivan's croaked.

Lucero nodded. "Indeed, I have." Once he was finished with the knife he set it back on the stand. "You see, it has the perfect shape and length to stimulate a special place inside a man, while its natural juices warm whatever it happens to be rubbed against." Grasping the root by the unpeeled end, he dipped it into the oil.

Ivan's eyes widened when the tip of the lubed root pressed against his crease. "You're not...ah fuck!" He bit his lower lip, his hips lifting from the bed, impeding Lucero's access.

"Now that won't do." Reaching behind him, Lucero loosened the bonds holding Ivan's legs. After repositioning them so Ivan's puckered star was exposed to his gaze, Lucero retied them. "Better. Just relax. I promise this will feel good."

Ivan gasped for breath, a bead of sweat running down his cheek. "You'd say that even if it burned like hell."

A chuckle escaped Lucero. "You're probably right." After lubing his fingers, he rubbed them over Ivan's anus. "Push out for me. Let me in."

Ivan gave a tortured moan and obeyed, the muscle relaxing.

"Good boy." Before he eased any deeper, Lucero blew on Ivan's cock to distract him.

"Shit, so good." Ivan rocked, using his tied position to tilt his cock toward Lucero's face.

"Mmmmm." Unable to resist, he captured the flared crown and sucked it deep in his mouth, pulling his fingers out and replacing them with the root.

"Ahh." Ivan stiffened while a string of profanities spilled out of him. His cock thickened against Lucero's tongue, and more fluid coated his taste buds. Lucero hummed low in his throat, but continued, keeping the pressure steady until he sank the root deep inside of the moaning off-worlder. When he couldn't push it any farther, he paused, listening to the raspy sound of Ivan's breathing. The man was no longer cursing. Instead, he trembled and sweated. Scanning Ivan's vitals by placing a finger on the artery inches from his face, he quickly assured himself the man hadn't gone into shock. His eyes widened as the readings came back to him. While Ivan was very close to coming, he was now floating on the edge of *caelum*.

Letting the cock pop out of his mouth, he rested his forehead against Ivan's thigh, searching for his self-control. Ivan being so close to the vault of heaven was like a straight shot of aphrodisiac to Lucero's system. He was about to come apart at the seams. Only the need to push his lover completely outside himself kept him tethered to reality.

Ivan clenched down on whatever the hell root it was Lucero had shoved up his ass. The slight burn only sent him higher. All he needed was a few more tugs and he'd come. Instead, as if from a distance, Lucero's mouth abandoned his cock. So close to release, he wanted to protest, even beg for the return of its wet embrace, but realized he couldn't find the words, let alone force them past his lips. It took a concentrated effort on his part to focus on the cyborg as Lucero crawled to his knees, his lips swollen and his amber eyes full of emotion. Something inside of Ivan shifted. This was the man who wasn't afraid to give him what he needed. The only thing imperfect was the clothing hiding Lucero's body from his gaze. He wanted the clothes off. He needed skin-on-skin contact to nourish the connection growing between them.

"Sir?" It took some doing. Even with effort the word came out raspy.

"Shh." Leaning over him, Lucero released him from his bonds. Then he helped Ivan roll over. "Up on your knees. I want to see that tight ass."

On the edge of something even stronger than the orgasm pooling in his balls, Ivan nodded and tried to balance on his knees. When he swayed dangerously, Lucero helped him redistribute some of his weight onto his hands.

"There you go." He ran a palm down Ivan's spine. "So beautiful, but it will even be more so when you carry my marks." After pressing a kiss to his shoulder blade, Lucero pulled back and tapped the root, sending it deeper. Ivan groaned as it rubbed over his prostate. The blend of tingling coolness from the oil and heat from the *aculeatum herba* was so addictive, he barely heard Lucero's next words.

"I made this for you out of the inner fronds of the *tuerentur*. They are supple and will send you flying."

"Flying?" At a glimpse of the many-stranded flogger Lucero held, he dug his fingers into the bedding and braced himself.

"Yes." The cool trail of the fronds across his back was his only warning. "Remember your safeword if you need it."

"Dahlia?" He was still trying to figure out why he might need it, when the first lash hit his ass. "Shit!" Pain radiated, but morphed into pleasure when Lucero pressed a kiss to the mark.

"Are you safewording?"

He shook his head, lifting his ass higher.

"Good. Just relax into it, Ivan."

A whistle cut through the air, and the other side of his ass lit up. He groaned, every part of him drawing up. His cock leaked as he begged for more. "Please."

"I will. In time."

Lucero started a steady rhythm of alternating kisses from the flogger with those from his mouth, until Ivan was ready to float free of his body. The pain was wrapped so tight in the pleasure, he couldn't separate the two. He squeezed his eyes shut when Lucero's hand found his erection, adding another layer to his pleasure and pushing him closer to something he'd never experienced before. He tried to groan, he tried to rock forward, he even tried to beg, but Lucero kept control. With one long, slow pull on his cock and a final hard slap on Ivan's ass, he sent him over the edge.

"Come, my love. Find *caelum*."

Ivan gave a broken sigh, his hips jerked as pleasure buffeted him, and he sank into a comforting darkness where nothing mattered.

Chapter Seven

Sprawled across the bedding, Ivan's long limbs took up every inch of real estate as he softly snored. Lucero knew he should take the man back to the living room, insist he continue to sleep alone, but deep inside him, he could already feel the strengthening bond between them. Nearly complete, all it needed was the final night, the *sacra fide*. If things were different, Lucero would relish, even anticipate their joining with great pleasure.

But they're not. When he looks at me, he still sees a machine, something not human or worthy of love.

The brutal truth confronted him. Despite sending Ivan to *caelum*, he couldn't help but remember their conversation over the previous morning's breakfast. To Ivan, he was a means to an end, the *tribus noctibus*, something he had to endure to get what he wanted. It saddened Lucero. The ritual should be a time of pleasure and starting anew. Instead, he'd foolishly turned it into nothing more than a pawn in a game. His soul cried out for Ivan. The off-worlder could've been the answer to his prayers, but, with his own words, he'd damned himself. Because, no matter how much Lucero's body ached to complete the ritual, to take the lover who now slumbered in his bed, it wasn't meant to be.

He raked his hands through his hair, wrestling with the need to strip his clothing away and join Ivan. His cock ached worse than he could ever remember. Not even during his mating with Vihaan had his body reacted like this. Unless he chose to dishonor the ritual, to masturbate and find his pleasure alone, he was trapped in hell. He would be unable to go forward, while fated never to return to the numb state he'd been in since Vihaan's death. But could he complete it, when Ivan would eventually leave? The question tormented him when he bent to cover the other man with the light sheet pooled at the end of his bed.

When a soft sigh escaped Ivan as he snuggled deeper into the pillows, Lucero clenched his jaw and took a deep breath. He couldn't do it again, couldn't go through the pain of losing another mate. He had to put a stop to the *tribus noctibus* before the bond was irrevocable. After taking one last inhalation to savor the scent of Ivan's release, he slipped from the room. *This has to stop.*

The sound of the outer door shutting drew Ivan from his slumber. The urge to remain in his warm cocoon was tempting, but old habits die hard. He never slept in another's bed. Opening his eyes, he sat up and let the sheet fall to his waist. He swung his legs over the edge, wincing when the move put pressure on his sore ass. Standing, he reached toward the ceiling, stretching every muscle in his body. Twisting, he caught a flash of motion from the corner of his eye. Hoping it was Lucero, he turned his head only to see his own reflection in the free-standing mirror next the dresser. At a glimpse of red on his ass, he moved closer, his curiosity roused. After positioning himself to best see, he peered into the reflective surface.

A low moan passed his lips at the sight. Thick, cherry-pink stripes decorated his ass and upper legs, the marks standing out against his pale skin. He skimmed his fingers over a long one that wrapped around his outer thigh and toward his hip. A tingle of pleasure mixed with a twinge of pain jolted through him, making him catch his breath. He hadn't expected it to feel like that. His cock stirred. Once again, Lucero had sent him over the edge, but taken no pleasure for himself.

"Well, that's about to change." He straightened. "Power exchange or not, it's not fair. I'm going to make him come before the night is over." Striding naked from the bedroom, he moved toward the living room. But after a thorough search of living room, kitchen, halls, and bathroom, he couldn't find the cyborg. Then he noticed the door leading to the hot spring was ajar.

He slipped through the opening and retraced his route, until he found himself standing at the edge of the pool. Steam rose in wispy curls. However, the soft gurgle of water couldn't disguise the low masculine groan. Inching closer, he caught his breath at sight of Lucero standing in the pool. The foam of the pool lapped at the cyborg's thighs, while dewy droplets of moisture clung to his tapered waist and lightly muscled torso. But the hand moving up and down Lucero's thick erection had Ivan's mouth drying out.

A long, tortured sound, followed by Lucero reaching up to pinch his own nipple, sent a flood of lust to Ivan's groin. The idea the other man liked a bit of pain with his pleasure made Ivan hard. *What else will make him moan? My teeth? Would he cry out if I did the same to his dick?* The litany of questions swarmed him until he was trembling with need to find out.

"Fuck, *amans*." A hoarse plea as Lucero's hand frantically worked his cock. "Need to come."

On light feet, Ivan approached the pool, his gaze taking in every nuance of pleasure and pain consuming the man before him. He drew closer as Lucero labored to bring himself off. The jerky motions, closed eyes, grimace, and rocking of Lucero's hips told their own story—the cyborg was close to release. Even as hot as he found the idea, Ivan couldn't help but be pissed the man left his side to seek his pleasure alone. Was he that repugnant, or did Lucero refuse to allow it because he'd been hurt by the death of his first mate?

Using the sound of the frothing water to cover his movements, Ivan slipped into the pool behind him. He bit his lower lip to keep from moaning when the hot water stroked over the fresh welts on his ass and upper thighs. He pushed away the sting and focused instead on the man in front of him. Close enough to lick up the bead of sweat running down Lucero's cheek and inhale the heady scent of his arousal, Ivan waited for the right moment to touch the cyborg.

"Fuck, I can't." With his eyes still closed, Lucero's hand dropped away while a tremor shook his frame.

"But I can." Ivan whispered the word against the skin below Lucero's ear before wrapping his fist around the broad shaft.

"What—" Lucero jerked against him but stilled when Ivan sank his teeth into the thick muscle across the top of his shoulder. His warning for the other man not to resist was clear.

Using the rhythm he himself enjoyed, Ivan alternated fast and slow strokes up and down Lucero's length.

"*Stop!*" Lucero grabbed his wrist. "I can't do this. I don't—"

Ivan growled his displeasure, but lifted his mouth. "I'll fucking sleep with you."

"Why?" The question barely reached his ears.

"Because this one-sided shit is gonna come to a stop." He nipped the crook of Lucero's neck. "Now, let go. I want to find out what you look like when you come."

"I...." Lucero wavered.

Sensing how close the cyborg was to release, Ivan began to whisper soft, naughty words. "Please, Sir. I need to feel you spurting all over my hand, to listen to your cries, to know I've given you the smallest amount of pleasure."

Lucero groaned, before his head tipped back to rest against Ivan's shoulder. The move gave Ivan a bird's-eye view of his hand working Lucero's cock. The tip, a little more rounded than his own, was a deep vermillion while a thin trickle of iridescent fluid leaked from the slit to coat Ivan's lighter-hued fingers.

"So fucking hot." Ivan stroked him faster while rubbing his own cock between the cheeks of Lucero's ass. "Please, Sir."

"*Amans!*" Lucero came with a stifled shout, his eyes squeezed shut and body trembling against Ivan's. Long bursts of creamy seed flowed from Lucero's tip to splatter on the water's surface. He had never seen anything as erotic. It made him want to come all over his Sir's ass, but he refrained, a small part of him longing for the cyborg's permission.

***

Fuck. Fuck. Fuck.

The litany of curse words kept repeating through Lucero's brain. He was so screwed. He'd never expected Ivan to follow him down to the hot springs. He'd assumed the man would sleep for a few more hours, and by then he'd have broken their emerging bond. Then he could've completed their third night without the resulting mating. *Or taken him back to the clutch.*

"Aren't you going to say something? Scold me for taking control?" Ivan nuzzled his ear, his arms tightening around him in an affectionate hug.

"No." He wouldn't blame Ivan for his own actions. *He'd* given in to the pleasure the off-worlder had offered. Unfamiliar with Lucero's customs, the man had no idea he'd just strengthened their emerging bond.

"Good." Ivan rocked against his ass, his hard-on slipping up and down Lucero's crevice. "Because even if you'd tanned my ass for it, I don't think it would've stopped me." Ivan's tongue teased the lobe of his ear. "I almost came with you."

Lucero squeezed his eyes shut. "You did?"

"Mm-hm." Ivan scraped his fingernails over Lucero's hipbones. "A man of my age and experience should have more control. Only one thing stopped me."

Lucero groaned as Ivan recaptured his sensitive dick and gave it a firm tug.

"Do you know what stopped me?" Ivan nipped his ear. "You didn't give me permission."

"*Amans.*" Lucero couldn't help the rasp of his voice when Ivan thumbed the head of his cock.

"But, more than anything, even my own desire to come, I want to see you do it again." Ivan released him then slipped around to kneel in the swirling water in front of him. "This time, I want to feel you come on my tongue."

A deep agonizing groan wrenched free of him when Ivan tried to seal his lips over the head of Lucero's dick. The only thing stopping him was Lucero's hand in his hair. Jerking his head back, Lucero struggled for control. He was the one in charge, despite his earlier lapse. "Stop."

Ivan froze, a puzzled expression crossing his expressive face. "You don't want a blow job?"

Lucero narrowed his eyes, trying to comprehend what the off-worlder was talking about.

Blow job?

"I'll take your silence as a no." Ivan moved to stand. "Damn, just my luck – the first man I've gone down on my knees for in years, and he doesn't want my mouth anywhere near his dick."

"I didn't say that." He pressed down on Ivan's shoulders, pushing the man back to his knees. "You have made rather free with your hands already.

Something I should've stopped. Despite the pleasure it would bring, I would be a fool to let you continue. I decide if I want to come in your mouth – not you."

Ivan looked up at him, understanding shining from his gaze. "I fucked up, didn't I? Went too far."

"Yes, you did. But I allowed it, so the blame falls at my feet. While you followed your instincts, it was my duty to guide you. To decide how far we go."

Taking a deep breath, Ivan lowered his gaze. "Understood, Sir. It won't happen again."

The man looked so forlorn, Lucero almost felt bad for denying Ivan when he knew both of them would enjoy it. Wrapping his hand around his shaft, he brushed the tip over Ivan's lower lip. "Open. I want to feel your lips around me."

Ivan didn't wait for him to repeat the order. His lips parted, then he sucked him inside the warm cavern of his mouth.

"*Ivan.*" Lucero gritted his teeth when the man's inquisitive tongue found the sensitive underside of his cock. Every brush of it, every pull of Ivan's lips, brought him closer to the edge. Threading his fingers through Ivan's short hair, he cradled the back of his skull. "That's it. Take it. Suck me."

Ivan made a muffled sound of agreement as Lucero thrust toward him. Sweat, which had nothing to do with the hot spring he stood in, broke out on his forehead, but Lucero was too wrapped up in the pleasure his lover brought with his wicked mouth. His breath rattled in and out of his chest, his thighs trembled, and his balls drew up tighter with each hard pull of Ivan's mouth. Poised on the edge of another amazing release, he began to pant. He wanted to come, but would the man accept his release? Or would he pull away? Vihaan had never swallowed, claiming as a royal, it was beneath him, and he'd never be able to bring himself to do so. In the end, it mattered not. Lucero had respected his hard limits. However, he would not take the choice away from Ivan. Lucero released his head and tried to pull back. His lover growled then glared up at him. As if he was depriving him of a treat.

Lucero panted. "Please remove your mouth. Unless you want to taste me, you need to pull back."

Instead of answering him, Ivan clasped his hips and jerked him forward, his tongue lashing at Lucero's trapped cock. Then his *amans* pulled back and rubbed Lucero's cock across his face. The sheer eroticism of witnessing Ivan submit to his urges gave him the extra push he needed. With a hoarse shout he spurted his release all over Ivan's face. Before he finished, Ivan extended his tongue and caught the remaining weak bursts. With appreciative moans, Ivan continued to milk his shaft, riding out Lucero's pleasure. It made him shake. Each time he fisted Lucero's length only drove him higher until he almost touched *caelum*. By the time the off-worlder surged to his feet, sending water flying, all he could do was cling to Ivan's shoulders as his lover picked him up. He'd never experienced such brutal pleasure once, let alone twice in such a short time. But when Ivan carried him out of the hot springs, cradled against his chest like a baby, Lucero stirred.

"Shhh, I've got you." Ivan's voice rumbled under his ear, as he paused next to the branch where Lucero had hung his towel. "Grab the towel, sweetheart."

Lucero's eyes stung with unshed tears at the tenderness displayed on Ivan's face. It wouldn't take much to forget his misgivings about surrendering his soul to the off-worlder. With trembling fingers, he reached out and snagged the cloth. He opened his mouth to order the man to put him down when Ivan arched a brow at him.

"If you're going to say something to piss me off, don't. It's late and we both need a solid eight hours of shut-eye. We're going to bed."

When Ivan shouldered past the low-hanging branches, managing to protect him in the process, Lucero stared up at his lover's profile. There was new softness along his jaw, as if something, or someone, had put him at ease. It dawned on him as Ivan carried him up the sloped path to the entrance to his home that, for once, he was seeing a hidden part of Ivan.

"Grab the door." Ivan's order was soft but not impatient when Lucero fumbled with the latch.

Once inside his home, he expected Ivan to put him down, but instead he carried him all the way to his bed. Once there, he let Lucero slide down his body, until he stood before him. Taking the towel, he began to briskly dry Lucero off, before attending to his own body.

"Dry enough." Ivan stated around a yawn. "Up you go." He pulled the sheets back after straightening the pillows.

Lucero couldn't help but stare. Ivan turned and glanced down at him. "What? Just because I've been letting you call the shots in the bedroom, doesn't mean I'm going to let you control everything we do outside of it." He pointed to the bed. "Now get your sexy ass in bed, before junior decides he wants an encore."

"Junior?" He cocked his head. "Who is this junior?"

Ivan chuckled, gesturing to his groin. "Junior." His smile faded. "I think we both need some sleep before we take this to the next step. Wouldn't you agree?"

Licking his lips, Lucero gave a brief nod, before turning and climbing onto the bed. Seconds later the bed rocked. A soft hiss escaped Ivan as he settled on his back.

Lucero pushed up on one arm. "Are you okay?"

Ivan's rueful grimace told its own story. "Forgot about my ass. Don't worry about it. Now that I'm settled, it doesn't hurt. Come here." He held his arms out, but when Lucero hesitated, he frowned and let them drop. "Unless, you don't want me to hold you as you sleep."

Lucero chewed on his lower lip while trying to decide what exactly the man was talking about.

"Look, don't wear your lip out. You were the one who wanted me here. If you don't want me touching you, fine." He rolled to his side, giving Lucero his back. In the dim light of the room, he could see the pink marks decorating Ivan's ass. How could they have been so close earlier and now be so far apart? How did he create the breach, the distance between them?

"I—" He reached out to touch Ivan.

"Don't worry about it. I promised to sleep with you. I'll keep to my side of the bed, and you'll keep to yours. Good night."

At the finality in his tone, Lucero lowered himself back to the bedding. How the hell had he fucked this up?

Chapter Eight

"Lucero, baby, you got to let go...." The soft words barely penetrated Lucero's subconscious.

"Hmmm." He mumbled, burying his face deeper in his pillow. It smelled wonderful. Just like his partially bonded mate. But when had feathers become so firm? He couldn't rouse himself enough to figure it out.

"Come on, I'll be right back. Swear. Just let me up. I got to take a leak." The pillow moved under his cheek. He growled and tugged it back. It was his pillow, and he wasn't sharing. "Mine."

"So you say. But your pillow is gonna get you wet if you don't let me up."

"Tired," he muttered, knowing Ivan was trying to convince him of something, but he was warm and sleepy. He rubbed his face against something like warm skin, drifting away again....

"Damnit, Lucero!" The frustrated tone cut through the haze of sleep. "Let go. I swear, for a man who doesn't like to cuddle, you're worse than a damned octopus."

Lucero's eyes flew open, as he was rolled over onto his back, his brain trying to engage. Something was off. Even with Ivan hanging over him, he'd never been so comfortable in his life. For the first time in his memory, he wanted to remain in bed. This lethargic euphoria was foreign to him. He usually sprang from the bed ready to start his day. He lifted his head to gaze up at Ivan, who'd pushed up into a sitting position. "What?"

"I said you're worse than an octopus." Ivan twisted and used an extended finger to push a piece of Lucero's hair back. "You know, the eight-legged sea creature?"

He stared blankly, his brain still struggling to come back on line. Had the release Ivan had given him the night before fried something? "Eight-legged creature? Where?"

Ivan chuckled. "Seems someone is a bit out of it this morning. Or, at least, I think it's morning. All I know is I woke up with you wrapped around me like a blanket, and I have to piss." He gave Lucero a nudge with his hip as he untangled their legs. "So why don't you keep the blankets warm, and I'll be right back. I could go for a few more hours of sleep once my bladder quits bitching at me."

Lucero scrambled into an upright position. "I'm sorry, I didn't mean...."

Ivan shrugged off his concerns and swung his legs over the edge of the bed. "Don't worry about it."

All Lucero could do was gawk, as his lover disappeared into the bathroom. He'd fucked everything up. If his Siserian mate, one of his own people, didn't like being touched at night, he could only imagine how the off-worlder felt about it. Hadn't Ivan said he didn't like sleeping with men? And from the way Ivan had woken him, he'd done more than touch. He'd used the man as his pillow. Mortification flooded him. How the hell was he going to fix this? Ivan would be well within his grounds to refuse the third night. To be so close to claiming the man as his, he was now terrified he would fuck it up and Ivan would leave him. By the time Ivan returned and slipped between the sheets, Lucero had worked himself into a lather. He resisted the urge to curl up next to Ivan when the off-worlder patted the spot next to him.

"Come here, baby."

The lazy drawl sent sparks of pleasure through Lucero, but he shook his head. "I'm sorry, I shouldn't have...I was sleeping...."

Ivan narrowed his eyes, reached out and wrapped his hand around Lucero's wrist then jerked him forward. Lucero gave a muffled *oof* with his nose buried in his lover's chest, and one of his legs trapped by Ivan's. He tried to push up, but the larger man swatted him on the ass. "Stop it."

"But—"

"But nothing." Ivan pulled him closer, his arm draped over Lucero's hip. With his free hand, Ivan cupped the back of his head. "No more protests. Just let me hold you, while we sleep." He pressed a kiss to Lucero's temple. "Morning will come soon enough."

"Umm, okay." He wanted to protest, but laid his head down on the arm under his head, his nose touching Ivan's chest. A deep inhale brought Ivan's scent, rubbing his face against the warm skin, his earlier contentment returned.

A chuckle shook Ivan's chest. "Cut it out. That tickles. Besides, you remind me of Luci-belle when you nuzzle me."

"Luci-belle?" Lucero let the name roll off his tongue, wondering if he should be jealous. "Who?"

"My Satan-spawned cat. You'd love her. Too bad you'll never get the chance." Ivan's hand stroked up and down his back. "Now, hush."

Savoring the soft strokes along his spine, Lucero couldn't get Ivan's words out of his. *Too bad you'll never get the chance. He still expects to return home to a place I can't go.*

***

When Ivan awoke several hours later, it was to an empty bed. Pushing up on one arm, he let loose a roar as the sheet pooled to his waist. He was sick of waking up to finding the man gone. "Lucero!"

Seconds later, Lucero walked out of the bathroom, fully dressed with boots on his feet. "Why are you yelling, off-worlder?"

Ivan frowned. "I woke up alone again. You know for a man who wanted me to sleep with him, you're becoming quite adept at sneaking away once I fall asleep. If I didn't have such strong self-esteem, I'd think you found my presence distasteful when we're not having sex."

Lucero's cheeks reddened. "It has nothing to do with sex, or your company being distasteful, Ivan. I set your clothing on the foot of the bed. I suggest you get dressed. If we're leaving today, we need to depart soon, or risk the forest at night."

"Where are we going? I still owe you one more night before we return."

Moving toward the dresser, Lucero picked up the short-bristled brush and pulled it through his hair. "I decided I don't want the last night."

"What the hell do you mean you don't want the third night? Weren't you the one who set the terms of our bargain?" Anger rose in Ivan's stomach. "Now you want to back out? Why the hell did you agree to return with me if you didn't want all three nights?" He tossed the blankets off his legs. "Or did you think I'd turn tail and run after what happened last night?"

Lucero set the brush down. "I wasn't sure what I expected when I made the bargain. I shouldn't have turned something as sacred as the *tribus noctibus* into a part of the queen's game. I'm sorry I put you in such a position." He glided toward the door. "So, once you get dressed and we've had breakfast, I'll return with you to the royal clutch." He took a deep breath. "I'll remain there, so you may go home. I've been alone for far too long if I can resort to such measures like blackmailing you. Perhaps I need some humility to remember what is truly important."

Desperation entwined with Ivan's anger, he rushed at the door, slamming it one-handed to keep Lucero from leaving. "Like hell. I promised you three nights. And I don't go back on my word."

Lucero twisted around to face him. "And you're not. I am. Now, please remove your hand so I may go make breakfast."

"No." Ivan clenched his jaw. He wouldn't let it end like this. Not without finding out if he could fully submit to Lucero.

"I won't argue about this. Remove your hand, or I will."

Sensing the finality in Lucero's voice, he changed tactics. "Just tell me why you changed your mind. You, at least, owe me that."

"Why does it matter? You will get what you wanted, to go home. And you won't have to endure the *sacra fide* to get it."

Confused by the cyborg's turnabout and more than a little pissed, Ivan narrowed his eyes and pressed his naked body up against Lucero's. He rubbed his bare cock over the light fabric of the other man's pants. "Does this feel like I'm *enduring* anything?" He leaned in until his lips were centimeters from Lucero's. "You whetted my appetite over the past two nights with those foreplay games, and now you want to withhold the main course? Back home we have a name for guys like you, and it's not nice."

"Better to be called names than be saddled with an unwanted mate."

Pain struck hard, wilting his erection. He refused to force himself on a man who didn't want him. "Fine. We'll go."

Lucero's breath caught and he nodded, his lips almost brushing Ivan's. Beyond tempted, Ivan reacted without thought. He leaned closer, desperate for at least one last taste. He crushed Lucero's mouth under his, running his tongue over the cyborg's full lower lip. When Lucero refused him entry, he growled. "At least give me one more real kiss before you take my ass back."

Placing his hands on Ivan's chest, Lucero pushed him away. Ivan swore softly, stumbling backwards. The expression on Lucero's face was impossible to read.

"I can't." He yanked the door open and was gone.

Left alone in the bedroom, Ivan wanted to hit something—hard.

***

By the time Ivan made it to the kitchen, nearly an hour had passed and he wasn't any calmer than he'd been when Lucero walked out. If anything, he was angrier. Which was never a good thing because, when he got angry, he became as vicious as a junkyard dog. Marching into the kitchen, he prepared himself for battle, but was sadly disappointed when all he saw was a plate of steamy food and a single folded piece of paper. Snatching it up, he glanced at what he assumed were words scratched across the surface. He scowled at the unreadable message before tossing it on the table. "Fucker, eventually you have to come back."

He sank into the chair and began to eat his breakfast. If they were indeed leaving, he would do so on a full belly. He was a little over halfway through his meal when he heard the door behind him creak. Figuring it was Lucero, he continued to shovel his food into his mouth. He wasn't going to give the cyborg the satisfaction of acknowledging his presence. But as long seconds stretched into minutes with the heavy stare focused on his back, he was ready to burst. He was just getting ready to turn and confront Lucero when the cyborg appeared in front of him and froze.

"Don't move."

"What? You told me to get my ass in gear to leave, and now you're telling me to sit still." Ivan pushed back from the table and rose to take his empty plate to the sink, when Lucero tackled him. The sudden strike of the fangs burying themselves in the wood of the table, not inches from where he had been sitting only moments before was scary. But not as scary as Lucero rolling free of him, and launching himself at the nearly fifteen-foot-long snake. A grotesque shade of crimson scales dotted by violet-and-gray splotches covered the reptile from head to tail. The sucker had to be at least eighteen inches in diameter. He'd never seen a snake so big in his life. Not at the zoo, not even on the Discovery Channel. Whether it was its huge size or the spiked tail it sported, Ivan was scared out of his damned mind. He was horrified even more when the snake began to swing its deadly tail back and forth.

"Watch the tail!" he shouted, but was unsure if Lucero heard him or not. Ivan cursed and scrambled to his feet as the cyborg and snake crashed into the closest wall. Several paintings fell to the floor. After a quick scan of the room yielded nothing he could use, he darted into the kitchen. Yanking out drawers, he frantically searched for something, anything to help level the playing field. He finally found a long, curved blade and raced back from the kitchen to find the snake half-coiled around Lucero's neck and chest. The cyborg's face turned a decidedly blue hue as he gasped for air.

"No!" Raising the knife, he ran at the snake. He slashed at the nearest coil, while trying to avoid both its lethal fangs and tail. An ungodly hissing escaped the serpent as it twisted back, its beady, dark eyes locked on him. "Come on you bastard. Let's play." He dove to the left when it reared back to strike. It missed him by just a few inches, hissing its displeasure as it jerked its fangs free of the hard wooden floor. "That's right. You missed, asshole." He swung hard with his left hand, punching the snake on the side of the head. He danced back out of the way, but not before slicing at another coil of reptile muscle wrapped around Lucero. This time, bright-orange blood spurted through the air. It stung when it hit his skin, but he ignored it. He wouldn't let a little pain get in the way of saving his love. Lashing out again, he dug the knife deeper. The reptile screeched and tried to move away, dragging Lucero with it.

"No, you don't. You can't have him. He's mine!" Holding tight to his knife, he jumped on the snake, aiming in front of Lucero's body, and landing a few inches behind the creature's head. He groaned as the serpent tried to buck him off. In desperation, he pulled his arm back then thrust forward, burying the knife deep in the snake's skull. The dying beast surged forward one last time before falling to the floor, its coils gradually going limp.

Panic riding him hard, he climbed over the snake to Lucero. He shoved and pushed at the bits of dead serpent still wrapped around his lover, until he finally managed to drag Lucero free. Kneeling, he pulled him across his lap, alarmed the cyborg wasn't breathing. "No. Stay with me!" He tipped his lover's head back, squeezed his nose, covered Lucero's mouth with his own, and began CPR. Whether or not it would work on a half human, he didn't know, but he had to do something. He couldn't lose the man, cyborg or whatever he was. Ivan had fallen in love with him.

He lifted his mouth, slid Lucero down to the floor flat on his back, and began chest compressions. "Come on, breathe, dammit." Then returned to breathing into Lucero's mouth.

This time, when he came up, intent on another round of chest compressions, Lucero came alive. He clutched the back of Ivan's head hard, and turned what had been simple CPR into a torrid kiss. His tongue battled with Ivan's, his fingers sinking deep into Ivan's hair at the nape of his neck. With a soft moan, Ivan gave in, leaning forward and giving up control of not only the kiss, but their situation as well. Euphoria swamped him. Lucero was alive. Nothing else mattered

When Lucero released his lips, Ivan straightened and pulled the cyborg up into a sitting position.

"Did you mean it?" Lucero asked in a hoarse voice.

"Mean what?" Ivan stared at the huge dead snake.

"That I was yours? Or did I dream it?"

Ivan sighed. "Yeah." He closed his eyes for a moment in an effort to accept the truth. There would be no going back for him. "Whether you return to the royal clutch today or decide to complete the tribus noctibus tonight, you're mine. I won't leave you."

Chapter Nine

Lucero stepped back to admire his handiwork. In front of him and just to the left of his bed, Ivan stood on his tiptoes, back flush against the wall, with his arms extended above his head. A long tether ran from a hook several feet above him to the well-padded cuffs which encircled the off-worlder's wrists. His chest rose and fell erratically. His thick erection swayed and tempted Lucero with each move. After their close call, all he wanted to do was fuck the man and reassure himself he was unharmed. He still couldn't believe Ivan had taken on the *vipereum coluber* to save him. It had been a foolish move. *But I'll deal with his foolishness in a bit. First....* "You are here of your own accord?"

"Yes, sir." The reply was soft.

"And your word that stops it all?" Lucero twirled the flogger he'd retrieved from the top of his dresser between his fingers. It amazed him, after all his excuses and good intentions, they were still embarking upon the final night of the mating ritual. His plans to take Ivan back to the clutch had fallen by the wayside after the attack and Ivan's subsequent confession. The need in the other man's voice had melted any thought he'd had of resistance. Instead he'd taken Ivan by the hand and led him back to his bedroom.

"Dahlia, sir." Ivan laid his head against his raised arm.

Stepping closer to his man, Lucero let the strands of the flogger brush over Ivan's shoulder. "You will use it if the *sacra fide* becomes too much."

Ivan nodded. "It won't. I trust you, Sir."

Steeling his heart against the spreading warmth, he gave a few experimental swings. Once his arm was warmed up, he schooled his expression. "However, what you did today was foolish. You could've been hurt, *amans*."

"I couldn't let you—"

Sharp *pop* as the flogger's strands, meeting the skin of Ivan's chest, dragged a low groan from his man. "Unacceptable. If you are mine, you *will* take better care of yourself. There will be no more risking yourself needlessly, as you did today."

Ivan hissed, his cheeks flushed. "It was choking you. I'm supposed to do nothing while you die, Sir?"

He landed another blow to Ivan's tight abs, loving the way his lover swayed forward, his bonds the only thing keeping him upright. "I'm a cyborg. I can hold my breath longer than the average human. You endangered yourself."

A gasp rattled free of Ivan. "How was I supposed to know? You keep telling me you're a man. Your face turned blue. I had to save you."

Pleasure at his man's acknowledgement of his humanity surged through Lucero. "Which is why I will let your infraction's punishment end with the two strikes you've already taken, if...." He flicked the strands across Ivan's pecs, the strike light.

"If what, sir?" He wrapped his fingers around the chains, the move causing his chest muscles to flex.

"You promise to never do it again." He tipped Ivan's chin up with the handle of the flogger. "Twice, you've interfered during a battle. You've been fortunate and come out unscathed." He noted the silent protest in Ivan's blue eyes. "I've dealt with the creatures of the An'tealan Forest long before I fled to her embrace after Vihaan's death. You trust me with your body. Now, I need you to offer me the same trust when it comes to your safety."

Ivan's nostrils flared, his gaze seeking Lucero's. "Then, teach me. If I'm to remain with you, show me what to avoid, how to live in harmony as you do. Let me be a helpmate, not someone you have to protect and shelter. Don't treat me like a child."

Lucero froze. Ivan didn't want him to take control? Pain flared in the region of his chest. It was all good and well Ivan loved him, considering he was half in love with the stubborn human. But to give up control? He didn't think he could do it. Even after his slip-up in the pool, the need to dominate ran in his blood. He clenched his jaw. "You don't wish to submit to me?"

"This has nothing to do with submission." Ivan glared at him. "This has to do with day-to-day reality."

Lucero reached for the cuffs, ready to unhook his lover, but paused. "What do you mean by reality?"

Ivan blinked at him, and sighed deeply. "Think about it. You leave to go do whatever it is you do in the forest. What happens if another animal gets in the house or if one wanders too close to the hot spring? You would come back to find me dead or hurt." He tipped his head back. "Look, I'm not trying to usurp your dominance. In fact, it makes me hot, but I have to be alive to enjoy it."

He pursed his lips then gave Ivan a brief nod. "What you suggest makes sense." He cupped Ivan's cheek. "I will begin to teach you, on our way back, how to live as one with the An'tealan Forest. But when we arrive at the clutch, you shall acknowledge our mating in front of the queen. It will be the only way to keep her from punishing me." Leaning in, he brushed his lips across Ivan's. "She wouldn't dare harm the mate of the man who saved her clutch."

"Saved?" He mumbled the words, his eyes unfocused.

"Oh, yes. By bringing me back, you will most definitely have saved her ass. And deserve a reward. I can only hope you ask for my life." He nipped Ivan's lower lip. "But enough of that. I have a mating ritual to complete." Drawing back, he waited until the off-worlder relaxed into his bonds, with his hands loosely gripping the tether above the cuffs, before lashing out with the flogger. A bright-red welt appeared just below Ivan's collarbone.

"Shit!" Ivan swayed, his knuckles whitening around the tether, but his erection never wilted. In fact, a drop of pearly fluid slipped free to slide down the thick stalk.

"Breathe through it," Lucero advised, before he pulled his arm back. "You can handle it."

"Yes, Sir." Ivan inhaled, releasing a long breath as the next lash landed, this time on the opposite shoulder. "Damn." He tossed his head back, his muscles flexing as he pulled on his cuffs.

"Is that a good damn, or bad?" Lucero swung lightly at his future mate's wrists, allowing the tickling strands to tease the muscled forearms.

"Burns, but so good." He squeezed his eyes shut.

"Hmmm." Taking advantage of Ivan's lack of vision, he leaned in to lap at one of his lover's nipples. "As good as this?" He didn't wait for an answer before he sucked the pebbled flesh into his mouth. Using his tongue and teeth, he teased the captured nub while savoring the raspy moans above his head.

"Oh my god! Sir!" He jerked and tried to push closer to Lucero.

With one hand, Lucero caught his hip, using the other to rap his backside with the handle of the flogger. He lifted his mouth enough to reprimand Ivan. "Be still." Then he shifted his attention to his lover's neglected nipple. Circling it with the pointed tip of his tongue, he dug his fingers into the fleshy part of Ivan's quivering, flexing hip.

"*Iz lyubvi k vsego svyatogo.*" The hoarse need behind the strange foreign words washed over Lucero as he dragged the flogger up and down the crevice of Ivan's ass.

"You better not be cursing me, *amans.*" The warning was met by another spew of babble from Ivan when Lucero stood and pressed his clothed body against Ivan's naked one.

"No." Ivan opened his eyes, his gaze dazed with pleasure and need. "Praying for more."

A smile tugged at the corners of Lucero's mouth. "More of what? This?" He flicked the flogger at the small of Ivan's back. "Or more of this?" He wrapped his hand around the back of Ivan's neck and drew his head down, taking his lips in a kiss he hoped rocked his lover to the core.

More raw sounds were muffled against Lucero's lips, as he delved deep inside the honeyed warmth of Ivan's mouth. The tangy-sweet taste of the *mella* Ivan had drizzled over the bread he'd eaten was addictive. He wanted, no, he needed more of the tart flavor. But before he could indulge, he had to complete the final step of the mating ritual. He freed his mouth then nuzzled Ivan's scratchy jaw. "Are you ready to submit to me? To take my *ultrices* within you?"

"Damned if I know what you just said, but I'm ready to take anything you will give me." Ivan clenched his jaw. "You've teased me too well, Sir. I need you deep inside me."

Raging need combated with relief deep inside of him. With hands steadier than he expected, he unhooked Ivan from the wall. "Kneel."

Lowering himself to the floor, Ivan was so fucking horny he barely noticed the cool wood beneath him. He settled his weight a bit off-center to keep pressure off his bad knee, but never took his gaze off Lucero's smoldering eyes. "Sir?" He breathed the question out, his body yearning for something, anything, to indicate his lover was pleased with him.

"Good boy." The approval in Lucero's tone caressed him, his lover stroking the top of his head.

He closed his eyes, wishing he could hold onto the feeling forever.

"Free my *gallus,* Ivan. I want to feel you cradle the part of me that will soon enter your *asini.*"

When he hesitated, Lucero tugged his head back. Staring up at the tight planes of Lucero's face, he wet his lips.

"If I have to repeat myself, your ass will feel the lash of my flogger, before I take it."

Ivan savored the sting of his scalp for a millisecond before reaching out with his bound hands. Unfastening Lucero's pants, he gently freed the thick shaft he'd barely had time to get acquainted with at the pool. He extended his tongue and lapped at the drops beading the thick head.

"Still trying to take control, I see. I didn't tell you to use your mouth yet." Lucero groaned, his hips bucking once, before stilling. "Remove it until I give you permission."

Ivan moaned softly, but obeyed.

"Good boy." Lucero took a deep breath, then continued. "During the final night of the *sacra fide* you must freely take my *ultrices* within you twice to cement our bond. The first will be here, in your very talented mouth." He trailed his finger over Ivan's lips. "You must fully consume this time. Do you understand?"

Ivan's breath went ragged. *He wants me to swallow.* He barely contained his groan. While normally didn't let men spill inside his mouth, preferring to watch his lover's release spray, the desire to do so for the man who'd given him so much was strong. "Yes, Sir."

"Thank you, *amans*." Lucero guided his head toward his erection. "Open for me."

Parting his lips, he swiped his tongue over the head then sucked Lucero deep. He hollowed his cheeks, increasing the suction, bobbing his head in a short, almost choppy rhythm.

"Shhh, slow down. I'm not going anywhere." His lover's protest was raspy. "Tease me. Let me enjoy it. The last time was too fast."

"Mmmm." He mumbled his agreement around Lucero's cock. Keeping his motions smooth but almost lazy, he savored the hoarse sounds Lucero made. Hungry for more of them, he slipped his fingers under the lightly-furred scrotum and teased his taint.

"What are you doing to me, love? I've never...." Lucero bucked hard, nearly choking him.

You think that is intense? Just wait. Feeling the slightest bit naughty and more than eager to blow his lover's mind, he wiped the fingers of his free hand over the edge of his mouth, moistening them. Then he pressed firmly against his Sir's rosette, determined to give him a pleasure like none he'd ever known. He wanted to be even better than Lucero's last mate.

"What are you..?" Lucero's cock thickened even more against his tongue.

Humming low in his throat against a rock-hard shaft, he pressed deeper in and higher up until he found the small gland. Above him, Lucero shook and mumbled words in a language Ivan couldn't begin to understand.

"*Amans!*" Lucero jerked, and the first spurt filled Ivan's mouth. Without a thought about why he'd shied away in the past, he swallowed fast as release wracked the other man. Swallowing once, twice, even a third time, he took every drop into him. As it settled in his stomach, something wonderful but just a bit scary happened. He actually felt the emerging bond his lover had warned him about. Wonder barely had time to fill him when Lucero jerked him to his feet. "Enough." His hair disheveled, he was breathing hard. "I need you."

The cock he thought he'd just satisfied rose high and hard against Lucero's abs. "Sir?"

"Arms up." Lucero didn't wait for him to obey, but grabbed the tether and re-secured him to the hook. Once more stretched up on his tiptoes, Ivan barely had time to wonder what would happen next, when Lucero grabbed his left leg and hoisted it over his hip.

For a split second, he panicked, thinking he would fall.

Lucero growled. "I won't drop you."

The feral quality of his voice would've scared Ivan if he hadn't found it so damned erotic. Had he actually pushed the man in front of him to such lengths?

"I want your legs around my waist." He tugged Ivan's right leg up.

Instinctively, Ivan tightened his legs around him. He groaned when the cyborg stroked his cock, once, then twice, to gather enough pre-cum his fingers glistened.

"Relax," Lucero ordered.

At first Ivan wasn't sure what his sir wanted, until he felt the pressure against his anus. Tilting his head back, he let out a long moan when Lucero breached him. His ass greedily clamped down on the two fingers. "Sir!"

"Milk them. Just like you will do to my *gallus*."

Desperate for more, Ivan rocked forward, trying to push him deeper. Electricity jolted up his spine as Lucero pegged his gland.

A low sound of approval met his actions. "Damn if you aren't beautiful when you ride my fingers."

Gritting his teeth, Ivan lifted his head to meet Lucero's gaze. "More!"

Lucero narrowed his eyes. "Are you sure?"

"Dammit, if you don't fuck me, I'll...." He hissed.

"You'll what?" Lucero jerked his fingers free.

Ivan wanted to cry at the abandonment, but he was too busy trying to breathe through the slight sting as Lucero breached him. "Yes!" He tried to suck the man in farther, but Lucero's tight grip on his hips kept him immobile. "Please, Sir." He jerked on his restraints, uncaring that the cuffs cut into his wrists. Pushed beyond his limits, all he knew was he needed his sir to complete the bond before he went crazy.

"Shhh, we'll get there." Lucero's erection slowly forged deeper.

Ivan cried out when Lucero finally sank in to the hilt. "Yes. Fuck, yes." He squeezed his ass, massaging the cock inside it.

"Look at me, *amans*. Before we finish this, we have one last thing to do."

Focusing on Lucero took some doing, but he finally managed. And was glad he had. Nothing was sexier than his Sir with flushed cheeks and determination stamped on his face. In his palm, he cupped several small pieces of what looked like silver rods and even a disk. Ivan's lust-dazed mind tried to wrap around what his lover was holding.

"It is customary for the *praesul* to mark his mate. It's a sign of honor, and lets everyone know you are taken. Will you allow me to place this shield,"—he held out a silver disk with the center cut out of it—"around your nipple and close to your chest?"

Blinking, Ivan glanced between the shield and Lucero. "I'd love to wear it, but I don't know if it will stay...."

An amused grin crossed Lucero's face. "True...which is what these are for." He pinched two slender rods between his fingers. "I will have to insert these through your nipple."

Shock warred with surprise. He'd toyed more than once with getting his nipples pierced at home but had never gotten around to it. "You want to pierce me? While you're balls deep in me?"

Lucero bit his lower lip then gave a slow nod. "More than anything. Knowing you would take the pain to be mine makes me harder." He drew a deep breath. "I had these made for my mating with Vihaan, but he refused them during the *sacra fide*. Son to the queen, he felt it was below him to wear the mark of three, especially to a cyborg who wasn't even considered to be a man. So I packed them away until I met this sexy off-worlder who showed me I could have more. Will you accept them?"

Sensing the need behind Lucero's words, Ivan glanced at the items again, looked him in the eye, and gave a slow nod. He didn't know how the cyborg would manage it while embedded deep in him, but he trusted Lucero. "Yes."

Hunger flared in Lucero's gaze. "Thank you, Ivan. With this shield, I offer you the first mark. Like it, I shall protect you." Then he placed the brushed silver over Ivan's left nipple. Ivan shivered at the touch of the cold metal. He watched as Lucero unscrewed the small balls on either ends of the rods.

Lucero paused. "Before we continue, I can deaden the pain for you."

Confused, he tightened his legs around his lover. "Didn't you just tell me knowing I could take the pain to be yours makes you hard?"

Cupping Ivan's cheek, Lucero nodded. "It does, but it doesn't mean you have to. This relationship isn't just about me, it's about both of us. I can live without it, especially if I see the *insigne trium*."

Warmth filled Ivan. The idea Lucero would give up something that meant so much to him, for Ivan's comfort, made him want to endure it. "I want the pain, Sir."

"As you wish." He pressed the sharp end of the bar to the side of Ivan's nipple. "Breathe for me, Ivan. With this rod, I offer you the second mark and swear to love you with a firm hand."

Pain flared bright as the rod pierced him. Ivan hissed but refused to give in. He exhaled loudly when it suddenly stopped. He glanced down at his chest and watched as Lucero slid a U-shaped hoop on to both ends of the rod, before using the small metal balls to secure it. He'd never seen anything so.... "It's beautiful."

"It is." The possessive approval in Lucero's gaze warmed Ivan. "But not as beautiful as it will be." He held up another piece of metal, this rod shorter than the first and had a small ball similar to the other. "The *tertia* will hurt a bit more. I have to go through the center of your nipple to attach it to your rod."

"Finish it. Make me yours." Ivan kept his gaze on Lucero's as a sharper sting flared in his already abused nipple. The pain grew in proportion until his safeword trembled on his lips, when Lucero's voice reached through the pain and centered him once more.

"Relax, breathe through it. I'm almost done. With this *tertia,* I give you part of me, knowing until our deaths, there cannot be one without the other."

Then there was a twisting motion against his nipple.

"It is done." Satisfaction poured off Lucero. "Look at it, *amans*."

Glancing down at the piercing, his cock, which had softened during the piercing, hardened once more. The shield framed his pierced nipple, dual hoops, one perched at the tip of his nipple accented the one below his nipple. He'd never seen anything as sexy in his life. It would be a permanent reminder of his place in Lucero's life. Kinky thoughts about what his lover could do with such a piercing teased him, making him even harder. "Damn. Once it's healed, do you have small weights to hang off the hoops?"

Lucero chuckled. "Perhaps." He cupped Ivan's ass. "If you're good. But first, let's finish this. I need to fill you with my *ultrices*."

Ivan gasped when Lucero began to move inside of him, slowly at first then faster their need spiraling out of control. The intensity increased, especially when Lucero wrapped his hand around Ivan's cock. The pleasure competed with then grew until it eclipsed the pain. "Shit. Gonna come, Sir."

"Yes." Lucero growled. His hips thrust faster and faster, every stroke pegging Ivan's prostate.

He screamed, his orgasm broadsiding him. Pleasure, even more brutal than the previous nights, had him spending several violent arches of seed until his chest was covered. Then he floated free of himself, losing himself to subspace.

From a distance, he heard Lucero whisper "good boy" before heat filled his ass, coming deep inside him. Still floating, he barely was aware of Lucero withdrawing or freeing him from his restraints. Or of being lifted and carried to the waiting bed.

"Come back to me, *amans*."

Ivan opened his eyes to stare at his mate, who perched on the edge of the mattress, wiping down Ivan's body with a damp cloth. "Wow."

"Yeah, wow." Lucero settled next to him on their bed after pulling the sheet up to cover them. "Rest."

More tired than he could ever remember being, Ivan yawned. "Mmm'k...love you."

Lucero tightened his arms around him. "I love you, too."

Chapter Ten

"Are you ready to do this?"

Standing just outside the skirts of the royal clutch, Lucero glanced over his shoulder at Ivan. The sunlight glinted off the silver piercing adorning his mate's nipple. At his request, the off-worlder had unbuttoned his shirt. Lucero not only wanted to be able to see his mark, but needed everyone in his former clutch to recognize Ivan was his. "I guess so."

Ivan smiled down at him. "Let's get this over with so we can get back to our home and start our honeymoon."

Lucero couldn't help but chuckle at the hopeful tone. Before Ivan had explained it to him, he had never heard of the sacred ritual married couples did directly after they wed, or, in this case mated. But he was looking forward to it. The full day and night they'd spent in bed had flown by too quickly. Then he'd rousted his lover early, leaving no time to make love to his mate. Their quick mating at the river hadn't been enough. He wanted the trip back to the royal clutch out of the way, so they could return home and he could explore every inch of his off-worlder. "Horny, *amans*?"

Ivan groaned and tugged Lucero's hand to his groin. The hard length of Ivan's erection didn't surprise him.

"Didn't our coupling during our lunch break take enough of the edge off?"

"Doesn't matter." Ivan nuzzled his ear. "I've been watching your ass wiggle for the past two hours." Ivan wrapped his arms around him from behind, his hands diving under Lucero's cloak to grope him.

He groaned softly. "Don't tempt me. The clutch is too close. They'd hear your screams and come running." He leaned his head back against Ivan's shoulder. He loved the fact his lover was bigger than him. Ivan made a wonderful cushion, whether it was for a quick cuddle or a rambunctious fuck. His cock hardened as the memories of the past twenty-four hours flooded him. "Only I'm allowed to see you naked."

His mate squeezed him. "I know, but I can't help it. You're sexy."

"Let's go." He pulled away.

"That's probably a good idea. Before I'm tempted to do something that will get my ass spanked later. After you, Sir."

Lucero shook his head and pushed through the dense brush. Stepping onto the barely maintained path, he glanced around. Squat buildings with royal clutch's flags and banners still stood, although their color was faded. Smoke bellowed out of several chimneys, while a lone guard walked the ramparts before disappearing from sight. Lucero had hoped to time it so the queen didn't have any advance notice of their return. The longer she thought Ivan had been slaughtered when her guards never returned from the An'tealan Forest, the better. The element of surprise would keep her from planning an attack and might just be beneficial as a bargaining chip. "Just like clockwork. We have about ten minutes before the guard returns to the west wall. Thank the gods not much has changed since I've left."

Ivan made a sound of agreement before pushing the strap of Lucero's bag of meager belongings higher on his shoulder. The off-worlder had insisted upon carrying it, after they'd agreed to only bring the bare necessities with them. "Let's get this over with. I want to return to our home. How long do you think it will take you to create and administer the vaccine?"

Lucero shrugged as they kept close to the wall and followed it around to the north gate. "It depends on how aggressive the particular strain is. Perhaps only a few hours, if we're lucky. The wait to see if it's a success or failure can drag on. The last time I injected a new vaccine, it took nearly three days to show any progress and nearly two weeks before the virus went into remission."

"Well, I'm not planning on sticking around for two weeks. Just make the vaccine, administer it then we're leaving."

Continuing to move toward the main gate, Lucero shook his head. "Bossy thing. I'll remember that tonight, when I get you alone." Glancing around, he felt compelled to warn his mate. "But I need you to keep your wits about you. It shouldn't be long before the guards spot us."

"Got it." Ivan remained his shadow.

When they got within ten yards of the gate, a shout went up. "You there!"

Lucero masked his expression. Let the games begin.

**

Following their escort to the Great Hall, Lucero fought the urge to flee. Every microfiber of his being protested the idea of being back here. He didn't trust the queen, but he refused to go back on his word. Ivan had given him one of the greatest gifts he'd ever received, and he'd be damned if he reneged on his promise.

"I'm surprised to see you, Wizard. When my guards never returned, I assumed the forest got all of you." Queen Theria swept into the room, her thigh-high black boots tapping out a hard rhythm on the floor. She'd aged in the two years he'd been gone.

The dark circles under her eyes, only a suggestion when he'd left, were now a predominant feature of her oval face. He activated his internal scan, and took advantage of her close proximity to get an initial readout. He frowned at the results the scanner fed back to him. If left untreated, she would die. The parasites had advanced to a stage so high, even with treatment, he wasn't sure he could save her. How had she gotten so bad, so quickly? What had caused this level of aggressiveness? He was dragged out of his thoughts though when she stepped closer to Ivan.

"It's great to see you survived the journey, Ivan. I can't even begin to fathom how you survived, let alone managed to retrieve our medic unit. This particular unit can be difficult at best."

She completely ignored Lucero's presence when in the company of others, as she had always done. Part of him stilled when she lifted her hand to touch Ivan.

"Of course, we had a deal, which I intend to honor. I will have my advisors begin searching for a way home to send you home."

"Don't bother. I've decided to stay here with my mate." Ivan shifted away from her outstretched fingers.

A delighted smile crossed her face. "Wonderful! I can always use a man of your talents at the royal clutch. Perhaps, with a bit of time, my people, and a lot of your know-how, we shall restore the clutch to her former glory. So, tell me, who is your mate? Perhaps a woman from one of the other clutches? I'm assuming you must've have found your way to one of them, since you survived the forest. Just give me her name, and I shall send for her immediately."

Before Ivan could reply, Lucero cleared his throat. "Your Highness, you are ill. Will you allow me to take a sample of your blood?"

She pursed her lips then held out her hand. "See, such a stubborn and difficult machine. Never knows when to keep its mouth shut and let its superiors talk. Why my son found him so amusing is beyond me."

"Enough, madam." Ivan growled. "I will not let you insult Lucero in such a way. My mate is much more than a machine."

Queen Theria jerked her hand away just as he pricked her finger. Large drops of black blood fell to the floor, but she didn't seem to notice. He could easily read the anger coming off her, but Ivan didn't even seem worried about it.

"Ivan, I can certainly understand why a man of your intelligence and education would be fascinated by the LT-1789, but he's not real. He's nothing more than a fancy gadget my grandfather created to care for the royal lineage. However, if men are your thing, why don't you let me introduce you to some of my male royals who prefer a man's touch to a woman's? You shouldn't have to settle for a machine posing as a man."

"No. I don't want a different mate." Ivan crossed his arms over his chest. "I found the one I want."

She gave him a tight smile, her brow furrowed. "Well, you can't have him. As property of the royal clutch, he belongs to me."

"No, he doesn't." Ivan glared at her. "The only person he belongs to is me. He's my Sir." He unfolded his arms and made a show of pushing his shirt back to

161

expose his *insigne trium* piercing. "He's marked me. From my understanding, in your culture, this means there will be no other for me."

A low squeal of outrage escaped her as she lunged toward Ivan. Lucero tried to catch her, but, being closer to Ivan, she managed to grab his mate's piercing. Ivan cried out in pain as she twisted the metal in an attempt to rip it free of the skin on his chest.

"You dare touch my mark!" he growled, flinging her away from Ivan with a well-placed blow. She slid halfway across the floor, the hall echoing with a sharp thud as she came to rest against her desk. Then, he turned, and barely managed to catch his mate before Ivan fell to his knees. "I got you, *amans*."

The paleness of Ivan's skin worried him. As a newly bonded mate, to have anyone other than his mate touch his *insigne trium* was agony. Lucero's heart stalled when he felt something warm and wet soak through his shirt. Pulling back, he stared at the blood pouring down Ivan's chest. The beautiful piercing was gone and nothing more than a gory mess of torn skin remained. Anger filled him. She'd destroyed something she had no right to even touch.

"Poor Lucero. You've lived too long on your own. You've forgotten your place." She motioned to the guards who'd flooded the room.

Before he could even warn Ivan, two guards grabbed his mate, while four more surrounded him. Pushing at the hands keeping him from Ivan, he tried to free himself, fear running through his system like a potent drug. He had to get to Ivan.

"Stop struggling, or I'll have them hurt him." She yanked on Lucero's hair. "Once again, it seems I must remind you of your place." She lifted the small electrode attached to the chain around her waist.

He inhaled sharply, recognizing the item. Set on the lowest setting the damn prod hurt like a bitch, but at the higher setting, it could kill him. He could only pray she wouldn't want him dead before he fabricated the vaccine.

Still reeling from the pain of his now gone piercing, Ivan struggled to free himself. The guards on either side of him tightened their holds. He could only watch in horror as the queen pressed a thin compact rod against Lucero's shoulder.

"When will you remember you have no rights I don't give you, machine. Vihaan realized that when he refused to wear your mating mark."

Sparks arched, and Lucero jerked, his body convulsing as electricity surged through his body. Anguish rushed through Ivan, and he again tried to free himself. "No! Stop it! You need him to fabricate the damned vaccine!"

Theria pulled back. "You're correct, Wizard. I do." She nodded to the men holding him. "Shall we give the machine some motivation?"

A swift kick to the back of his knee sent Ivan sprawling to the floor. If it hadn't been for the grip they had on his shoulders, he would've sprawled face-first on the stainless steel. He moved to stand, but froze when the sharp point of a sword pressed against the back of his neck.

"I wouldn't move too much, Mr. Chugunov." She turned to the men holding Lucero. "Get him upright." She lightly slapped Lucero's face. "Enough of this. I need the vaccine. Make it, or your new *mate's* life expectancy will be cut in half, literally."

Relief flowed through Ivan when Lucero slowly straightened. His voice was hoarse, but it was the best thing Ivan had ever heard.

"Tell them to let go of me. I need a larger sample of your blood and one of the clutch's water supply."

She nodded to the guard. "Release him." She sat down at her desk and motioned Lucero closer. "Let's begin."

Ivan watched helplessly, as the cyborg first drew the blood then smeared it on the panel in his arm. A short time later, one of the guards came back with a glass of water. After taking a piece of paper off the queen's desk, he scribbled something down, then tested the water. If it wasn't for the dire situation they found themselves in, he would find Ivan's medicinal and creative processes fascinating. He could almost see the wheels spinning inside his Sir's brain. This was his mate's element.

Nearly an hour had passed when the queen surged to her feet. "I grow impatient. What's the verdict, machine?"

Lucero looked up from the paper in front of him. "The new virus is a mutation I've never encountered before. I'm not 100 percent sure which antidote to prepare. This strain of bacteria supporting the virus is more aggressive than any I've seen in the past. It's interesting, really—"

"Enough! Can you create a vaccine for it?" The queen stomped her foot.

Lucero slowly nodded. "Yes, but only if you let my mate go."

She narrowed her eyes. "You're threatening me?"

"No, bargaining with you. You want the vaccine, I want my mate removed from all harm. Send him back to his home world. Regardless of what you do with me, he will be safe."

"Why? You don't want him anymore?" She asked him, as Lucero pressed a few buttons on his arm. Turning to Ivan, she smirked. "Hear that, Wizard? Your mate is ready to give you up."

Pain unrelated to his torn flesh threatened to consume him. Lucero couldn't reject him. Not after emotion in his Sir's eyes when he'd claimed him. "No." He whispered the protest, but when Lucero stiffened, he knew it had reached his mate.

"Are we in agreement?" Lucero's voice lacked any emotion.

The queen nodded. "Of course."

"You'll have your vaccine shortly, once I return to my lab."

"There is no lab." The queen crossed her arms over her chest. "I had it dismantled after you left. Give me the list of ingredients and equipment you need, and I'll have one of the guards run to the dry storage."

Lucero's jaw clenched, but he scratched out the list and ripped it free of the book. "Here." He handed it to the guard.

Within twenty minutes, the guard returned carrying a tray full of small bowls, a pestle and mortar, various powders and crystals in glass vials, along with a decanter of what looked like water, and several needled syringes. He set everything on the edge of the desk. Lucero began to create the vaccine, his motions smooth and fluid. It wasn't long before he was filling the syringes. After tapping the side of the needle, he offered it to the queen, who then stabbed him with it. He stiffened then his body began to shake. Finally, he doubled over.

"What the hell are you doing? Why did you that? He doesn't have the damned virus." Ivan tried to stand, but was forced back down by the ever-present guards.

"Relax, Wizard. This is protocol. All new vaccines are tried on the machine before they are injected into any royal. If they don't kill him, then they are safe for human use."

"If you hurt him, I'll—"

"Enough, *amans*." Lucero wheezed, straightening. "It's safe."

Taking another syringe, Theria filled it then injected herself. After a few long minutes, a pleased smile crossed her face. "I'm already feeling better. Check me, machine." She held out her hand. Lucero once more took blood and scanned.

"It's killing the virus."

"Good." The queen looked at the tray. "Is there enough to treat the rest of the clutch?"

Lucero nodded. "Of course."

"Good work." Then she surged to her feet and pushed the rod against his stomach. This time Lucero did more than arch. He screamed and fell to the floor, his limbs twitching. "For your insolence, you shall eventually die—when I feel you've suffered enough." Then she bent over and hit him again, this time in the chest.

Ivan tried to break free of the men. "Lucero!"

"Control him!" The queen snapped, straddling Lucero.

"Let me go! Don't touch him, you bitch!" Anger gave him a surge of strength and he managed to free one arm then, with great effort, pushed to his feet. The guards cursed loudly. He almost made it free when he felt a blinding pain at the back of his head—then nothing as darkness consumed him.

Epilogue

"Lucero!" Ivan came to, his heart racing with the need to save his mate. He was flat on his back, staring up at a stained ceiling. For a second, he thought he might be back in the dungeon, but the hard wood against his shoulders, ass, and legs felt more like a chair than the stone floor. He untangled himself from the chair, when a familiar face peeked over the edge of the poker table. With his jaunty little hat, his thick bramble of a beard, and that big hairy spider perched on his shoulder, the storyteller stared down at him. He was back in Chicago at Paddy McFee's.

"Whoa, are you all right? Did you knock your head on the floor? Leaning back in chairs can be dangerous, young man."

Sitting next to the discarded chair, with his chest heaving, he glared up at Nicodemus. "Send me back. I have to save him."

"Send you where? Save who?"

"Lucero. You sent me to another realm. I found my mate on Krontos. He claimed me, but now he's in danger. The queen is going to kill him." He surged to his feet, but was so unsteady he had to catch himself on the edge of the table. Nicodemus held out a hand to steady him. Ivan pushed it away. "If you're not going to send me back then I don't need your help."

A crooked smile crossed the storyteller's elfish face. "I wish I could help you, lad, but I do not know what you speak of. I'm a mere storyteller. You just paid me to tell you the tale of Iron John. The idea I can send you anywhere is...ludicrous."

"Ludicrous." He tore at his shirt, exposing his chest. "Then how do you explain this?"

"Explain what?' The little gnome tilted his head.

"The blood, the torn flesh. That bitch tore Lucero's *insigne trium* off me. One of their most sacred symbols—"

"Forgive me, lad, but I see no blood." Nicodemus's gaze was sympathetic. "Are you sure you didn't dream this world?"

"Dream it. Of course there is blood." He glanced down and stared in horror. His chest was completely unmarred, not a single trace of blood or torn flesh. But he could've sworn....

"Christ, Iron Man, I knew you were ripped, but man, you don't need to give the rest of us mere mortals a complex." Dante appeared in the doorway, his fedora tilted at a rakish angle. "Damn, you don't look too good. Maybe you'd better sit down?"

"Perhaps the lad hit his head a bit harder than he realized." Nicodemus settled in the middle of the table, his gaze catching Ivan's. "Why not have your friend take you home? My tale shall wait for another day."

Shaken to his core at the idea his time with Lucero had been nothing more than a dream, Ivan nodded. "Maybe I should." He tried to take a few steps, but his knees buckled and he nearly fell.

Dante rushed forward and caught him. "Whoa, I got you. Come on, big guy, let's get you home. I bet Lucibelle is wondering where you are."

He nodded then straightened. "Yeah."

They were just walking out, when Nicodemus called out to him one last time.

"Lad?"

Ivan stopped. "Yeah?"

The little man stood, soothing out the wrinkles in his red tunic, before hopping down from the table. "If you had the chance, would you have let him go, this man of yours, if it meant he survived?"

Never see Lucero again? He thought about it for a moment. "Absolutely."

A wide grin creased the gnome's face. "Then perhaps you don't need the Iron John tale after all. You already know the meaning of humility." He reached in his pocket and tossed the gold coin back to Ivan. "I never accept payment for a tale never told."

Pocketing the coin, Ivan nodded to the gnome and let Dante guide him out of the back room.

***

Once Ivan arrived at his apartment, he cut Dante off at the door. "No need to come in. I don't feel dizzy anymore."

Dante crossed his arms over his chest. "Are you sure? I can at least feed the cat for you."

After raking a hand through his hair, Ivan shook his head. "Don't worry about it. I'll feed the little demon spawn. Besides I don't need you to get sliced up by her. She hates strangers."

"Okay, but do me a favor. If you feel the least bit dizzy or sick, call me. You know Ronan and I are only a few minutes away. One of the benefits of living in the same building. "

"Yes, Mother." Ivan rolled his eyes. "Now, get. Your man is waiting for you."

Chuckling, Dante held up his hands. "No problem, I get it. You want to be alone. I'm going. Talk to you tomorrow."

Before entering his home, he waited until Dante disappeared inside the apartment he shared with Ronan.

"Lucky bastard." He opened the door cautiously in an effort to keep Luci-belle from sneaking out. The little escape artist had done it more than once. He frowned though when no cat appeared. "Luci-belle?"

He placed his keys on the hook next to the door then wandered into the kitchen, thinking she might be curled up on top of the refrigerator, one of her favorite places to ambush him. But a quick check revealed no calico cat. Frowning, he took a single beer from the fridge door. "Damn, not even the cat wants to see me unless I'm opening a tin of her favorite food. Which reminds me, I better give the picky princess her food."

Pulling open the cupboard, he grabbed a can of moist food, along with the bag of her dry food. It didn't take long for him to dump a cup of dry food in a bowl and top it with the moist. After placing it on the floor for her, he called for her again. "Come on, Luci-belle. I know I've been gone all day, but let's be realistic, I gotta work if you want canned cat food and kibble."

When he didn't hear any tinkling of her bell, he wandered into the living room. "Did you get stuck on top the entertainment center again?" Standing on tiptoe, he expected to find two green eyes staring at him from the shadows. "Okay, I don't feel like playing hide-and-seek, cat."

"This precious girl wouldn't do that, would she?" a voice asked from behind him.

Spinning around, Ivan's heart almost leapt out of his chest. At the entrance to the hallway, Lucero stood, holding Luci-belle in his arms. "Sir?"

Lucero's gaze darkened, even as he continued to rub his hand down Luci-belle's back. "You were right. I do love her. She's such an imp."

"How...I mean...I saw you...the queen...she was going to...kill you." Ivan swayed dangerously on his feet, his mind racing with questions about how his mate could be alive and, even better, standing in his Chicago apartment.

After setting down the cat down gently, Lucero walked up to him. "That she did—after making me build another of my kind." He cupped Ivan's cheek. "But it was worth every iota of pain, because my death allowed me to cross into your realm, so we could be together." A frown drew his brows together. "Unless you don't wish me to be your mate? You've changed your mind because I couldn't protect you?"

A low growl built in Ivan's throat as he jerked Lucero up against him. "Mine." He tipped up the cyborg's chin with his finger. "Always." Then he covered his mate's mouth with his. By the time Ivan lifted his head, both of them were breathing hard. "Just try to get away."

Lucero wrapped his arms around him. "Never." Then he pulled back, his hands shoving up Ivan's shirt. His fingers traced over the untouched, beyond merely healed, flesh of Ivan's chest. "Amazing." He met Ivan's gaze. "When I woke up in your apartment, I had only the clothing on my back and these." He pulled the silver pieces of the *insigne trium* out of his pocket. "Will you let me mark you again?"

Lucero had such an earnest expression on his face, Ivan couldn't help but pretend to contemplate it. "Perhaps. But only if it's on a weekend, Sir."

"And why's that?" Lucero asked softly, rubbing his thumb over Ivan's lower lip.

"Because, for some reason, placing them on me makes you horny, and I don't want to have to worry about going to work in the morning."

His mate chuckled. "And when does this 'weekend' begin?"

Ivan smiled then took his Sir by the hand to guide him toward the master bedroom. He couldn't wait to have his mate in his bed. "Funny you should ask. It's Friday, which means I don't have to work in the morning."

~A Letter from N.D. Wylder~

First I'd like to thank you for taking the time to pick up my book. I had an absolute blast creating this twisted fairytale. Once I read the fable of Iron John, my muse whispered in my ear, why not send a Tony Stark kind of guy to an alternate universe and have him meet a sexy cyborg who will rock his world? Unable to resist I channeled my own Tony as I wrote Ivan's tale. So come along as Ivan explores the lush An'tealan forest, and a sexy cyborg named Lucero, who like Piper, will challenge his perception of himself as a man. As they enter the mating ritual, tension and lust will be plentiful, so be sure you have something icy to drink. In the end however, I hope you'll enjoy reading Don't Call Me Iron Man as much as I did writing it.

You may visit with N.D. at:
http://ndwylders.webzai.com/ndwylders/